HIGH PRAISE FOR KATIE MAXWELL!

THEY WEAR WHAT *UNDER THEIR KILTS?*

"Welcome back to the sidesplitting universe of Emily Williams. . . . [This is] a larky addition that won't disappoint teens hooked by the first book."

—*Booklist*

"A complete blast to read."

—*RT BOOKclub*

"A must-have book, as Emily's antics can not be missed."

—Erika Sorocco, teen correspondent
for *The Press Enterprise*

"Maxwell delivers a character that speaks her mind while making you laugh out loud. . . . [A] real trip."

—*The Barnes & Noble Review*

THE YEAR MY LIFE WENT DOWN THE LOO

"*The Year My Life Went Down the Loo* is a treat! Laugh-out-loud funny, full of sly wit and humor, poignant, realistic teenage angst, and expertly drawn characters, the book is impossible to put down."

—*Romance Reviews Today*

"Gripping, smart-alecky, shocking . . . and at the same time tender. A brilliant debut by Katie Maxwell!"

—*KLIATT*

"[R]efreshing. It's so true to life, dealing with an average teenage girl's issues instead of the mild and bland subjects covered in many other YA novels. Girls will laugh, sigh and squeal aloud as they embark upon Emily's journey."

—*RT BOOKclub*

"Girls of all ages will find themselves laughing out loud at Emily's crazy antics and experiences, but will also find themselves relating [to her]. A great start to a great new series."

—Erika Sorocco, teen correspondent
for *The Press Enterprise*

BEWITCHED

Seth stared at me as if I had frogs sitting on my head. "Didn't you hear me say I was cursed? That everyone I like ends up getting hurt?"

"Yeah, I heard you, but . . ." I made a face my mother always calls wry. " . . . I just don't think it matters. Even if you are cursed—and I don't believe in curses—you're still you. You're nice, and really sweet even when you frown, and I like you. A lot. I'm not going to avoid you, if that's what you think. Uh . . . unless you really don't want me to be around, and you're just using the cursed thing as an excuse, in which case—"

I swear to God, I didn't know what he was going to do until he was right there, his hands on my arms, his face blocking out the moon as I blinked in surprise. One minute I was standing there feeling kind of sick because I figured that he might just be using the curse to get rid of me, and the next minute his mouth was on mine, warm and soft and all sorts of other wonderful words that I suddenly couldn't think of because my brain stopped working.

KATIE MAXWELL

EYELINER OF THE GODS

SMOOCH NEW YORK

*My profound thanks and undying gratitude
to Leah Hultenschmidt, one of the hardest
working public relations managers around;
and Kate Seaver, an editor who shares
my love of guys with motorcycles.*

SMOOCH ®

July 2004

Published by

Dorchester Publishing Co., Inc.
200 Madison Avenue
New York, NY 10016

ISBN 0-8439-5378-0

Printed in the United States of America.

Visit us on the web at www.smoochya.com.

EYELINER
OF THE
GODS

ANCIENT MUMMY CURSE ENDED
BY INTREPID TEEN!

CAIRO *(JanNews)*: Sixteen-year-old American January James arrived in Egypt earlier this month and single-handedly solved a centuries-old curse attached to the mummy of . . .

"Crap. What was the name of the person who lived in the tomb?"

The woman sitting next to me on the bus pursed her lips and squinted her eyes at my notebook.

"Sorry," I said, sliding my hand over it so she couldn't read what I'd written. "This is confidential. I'm a journalist. Or I will be someday. I'm hoping to sell a couple of my stories about my time at the dig, so I'm sure you understand if I can't show it to you now. Do you get the *Shocking News Today!* here in Egypt?"

The woman, who wore a white head scarf called a hijab, flared her nostrils at me and looked away as if she'd smelled something bad. I did a covert pit-sniff check just in case my deodorant had given way on me after the long flight from Paris—the heat in Cairo was enough to strip the air from your lungs—but the Ps checked out okay, so I just figured that she must be one of the conservative women Mrs. Andrews had told me about in her "dos and don'ts of going to Egypt" lecture. Most of the stuff she had told me was about how to be polite in another country, but some of it concerned how women were treated.

"I'm not wicked or anything because I'm traveling alone," I explained to the woman. She didn't look very convinced. In fact, she tried to avoid my eyes, but I felt it was important that the first person I talked to in Egypt *not* have the wrong impression of me. Start off as you mean to proceed, my mom always says. "Mrs. Andrews—she's our school principal—told me that Islamic rules say that men aren't supposed to harass women they don't know, but some men don't pay attention to the rules and look for women traveling on their own, figuring they're slut city, but I'm not. Just in case you were wondering. I don't even have a boyfriend! My sister April tried to give me Stan, her old boyfriend, but I draw the line at hand-me-down boyfriends."

The woman's nose looked pinched, as if she were trying not to breathe while sitting next to me. She glanced around the bus, obviously looking for another seat, but it was standing room only in the airport-to-Cairo bus.

"There was this guy last year whom I really liked, a senior, and man, I'm telling you, he was all that and a bag of chips, but he didn't even know I was alive, and I heard later from my friend Mina that he went off to be a monk or something, so that's probably why he didn't notice what guys usually notice about me."

I peered down at my chest. Even wearing April's loose Big Apple-tee, my boobs were right there where anyone could stare at them. And guys did. The dawgs. Like I could help having big breastages?

"Anyway, Mrs. Andrews said that in Egypt I shouldn't make eye contact with unknown men, or be nice to them, or anything like that, but that it was okay to be nice to a woman, which is why I'm talking to you. Only"—I bit my lip and tucked my pencil into the spiral top of the notebook—"what if the woman I talk to is lesbian? Would that be the same thing as talking to a man? What if she's a weirdo, into all sorts of pervy things like bondage and stuff? Wouldn't that be just as bad as being nice to a regular guy? And what about gay guys? Are they okay to talk to? Man, this being-polite-to-people-in-a-different-culture stuff is hard when they don't give you all the rules."

The woman, her eyes now tinged with desperation, tried to slide away from me, but the bus was an old one, and there wasn't a lot of seat space, so she really didn't have anywhere to go as the bus crawled its way through downtown Cairo.

I looked at the woman a little more closely. "My name is Jan. It's short for January. And yes, before you ask, I was born in January. My dad named me. He named the last five of us, because Mom had run out of names by then. He died right after October was born, but it's okay, because I was only two, so I don't remember him or anything, and then Mom remarried Rob, who is really nice and can't have kids because he only has one noogie, so he got all ten of us with Mom. Rob's an artist, of course. Who else would marry my family?"

The bus swerved to the side, throwing the woman next to me up against my shoulder. She made a horrified gasping noise, and quickly dragged herself off of me, half rising out of the seat as she scanned the bus for somewhere else to sit.

I looked around, too, suddenly realizing that I had been so busy writing what was sure to be a killer story, not to mention reassuring my seatmate that I wasn't Jan the Wonder Ho, that I hadn't been watching for the stop the airport map showed was right next to my hotel. The bus, which earlier had been traveling down the busy downtown Cairo streets of offices and modern buildings, was now honking and swerving its way down a different part of town, where the streets were narrow, dark, and filled with as many people as cars. The old, scrungy buildings that lined the street were a solid mass of open-fronted stores overflowing with everything from leather bags to big brass things (water pipes?), wooden walking sticks, brightly patterned clothing and colorful scarves, jewelry, food, wicker baskets filled with who knew what, and a gazillion other things that I didn't have time to take in.

"Flash! You're lost, Jan," I said to myself as the bus slammed to a stop while a donkey was dragged across the street by a guy in a long white-and-black robe. Donkeys! Uh-oh—I'd gone from industrial, modern Cairo to something out of an old mummy movie in just the amount of time it took to tell a woman I wasn't a perv. "I'd better get out before I end up at the pyramids or who knows where," I muttered as I stuffed my notebook away in the bag that had been wedged between my feet. I hoisted all five hundred pounds of it, dragging both it and me into the aisle of the bus, groaning to myself about my luck in being so wrapped up in taking notes at the airport that I'd missed meeting the volunteer coordinator.

Worst-case scenario was that I'd have to walk. It couldn't be that far back to the touristy part of Cairo—I'd been gabbing for only a few minutes, after all. "And besides," I told the hijab woman's back as I followed her while she pushed her way out the door of the crowded bus, "I swore to myself before I left home that I was going to use this month in Egypt to lose all the blubber that my mother insists on calling puppy fat despite the fact that I'm not a puppy, and if I were, it would mean she was a b— Uh . . . never mind, I probably shouldn't say that word here. Mrs. Andrews said profanity was a big no-no. Hello? Mrs. Hijab Lady? *Bititkalimi ingleezi?* Poop!"

She didn't answer my question about whether or not she spoke English, but the way she melted into the crowd more or less answered the question. I slung my duffel bag strap over my shoulder and jumped out of the way when the bus started forward, coughing as the diesel fumes swallowed me in a blue-gray cloud of haze. I had to admit to being a bit worried about the fact that I was lost in a strange city.

"Come on, Jan, get a grip," I told myself as I started down the crowded sidewalk. "You want to be a journalist, and everyone knows that journalists always do exciting things like get lost in the middle of Cairo."

Someone grabbed my sleeve.

"Hey!" I whirled around and came face-to-face with a leering guy with ugly black and yellow teeth. He said something that I was sure wasn't nice at all. I shook my finger at him. "My principal told me about you! She also told me what to say: *Áram!* Evil!"

The guy blinked at me in surprise as I yelled the word at him, but I didn't wait to see how he was going to re-

5

spond. I spun around and started walking quickly the way the bus had come, weaving my way through the crowds and stacks of things for sale, dodging dogs and donkeys and small boys sitting with wicker baskets of food who yelled at me as I went by. The noise was incredible—people were chatting, laughing, yelling, singing, and calling to each other over the dull throb of traffic, the blare of car horns an underscore to the loud, high-pitched singing from someone's radio, all of which blended with a thousand other noises that you don't know exist until you suddenly find yourself stranded half a world away from your home.

My stomach growled as I marched down the street, the spicy odor of cooking meat wafting out from one of the shops. The smell of the diesel belching out of the cars that worked their way down the street was nasty, but there were other scents that were a lot more pleasant—musk and patchouli from an incense place, the familiar smell of oranges from a nearby orange vendor, and lots of nummy restaurant smells that had me swallowing back gallons of saliva and reminding myself that I was supposed to be on a diet.

"It's not fair," I muttered as I stopped in front of a store that had the most delicious-looking pastries displayed on a cart. "Here I am in exotic Egypt, and I'm not allowed to eat anything but water and ice cubes."

Two people nearby stopped to stare at me. Belatedly I remembered that Mrs. Andrews had said I should always have a companion when touring the cities, but I hadn't intended on having to walk through half of Cairo to get to the hotel. I moved on.

"It's like this," I said to no one in particular, practicing the excuse I'd offer the volunteer coordinator as I lugged my bag (evidently now filled with lead and anvils and other hard, heavy things that were slowly dragging my shoulder down) through the quickly darkening narrow street. " 'I got lost at the airport and missed the group connection to the hotel.' "

Oh, yeah, that sounded lame. Lame-o-lame. Lamer than George W. Bush in jogging shorts.

"Um . . . maybe this is better. 'Sorry I missed you at the airport, Ms. Sorensson, but I had to go to the bathroom really badly . . .' Ugh. No. She'll think I've got the big D if I say that. And I'd die if anyone thought I had the trots."

I came to a corner and paused. The street ahead narrowed even further, so no cars were able to drive down it, which, considering what I'd seen of Cairo drivers so far, was a blessing, but I was trying to retrace the bus's path.

"Okay, here's the deal—'I'm a journalist, and I was positive the guy in front of me at customs was a smuggler, so I had to hang around and take notes on him, and that's how I missed the meeting with you. . . .' " I sighed. "You know you're in trouble when the truth sounds weirder than fiction. You also know you're in trouble when you stand around talking out loud to yourself, especially when you have an audience."

My audience was apparently *not* appreciative of the fact that I had arrived in their city. A group of four guys in really ugly shirts lounging around outside what looked like a tobacco shop yelled catcalls across the street at me. The people walking around me gave me really unpleasant looks; even the women scowled as they tromped around me. Lost, alone, and without a good excuse for missing my contact at the airport, I turned to the left and tried to look innocent and not at all like a she-cat on the prowl for some lusty, busty action, praying all the while that I was heading in the direction of the Luxor Hotel.

"Moomkin almiss bizazeek?" The sneering voice, accompanied by a tug on my bag, had me spinning around, clutching the duffel bag tightly in case some of the street kids were thinking of doing a five-fingered rocket job on me. It wasn't the kids, though . . . it was the guys from the cigarette shop.

They were all pretty young, all but one in thin cotton shirts that looked like they were made out of the same material as my grandmother's kitchen curtains, and tight black pants. The guys weren't even cute, and if I have one rule in life, it's that the very least a guy who is going to hit on me can do is to be droolworthy. These guys weren't even remotely cute. They did, however, smell like they'd taken a bath in cheap men's cologne.

One of them, the one closest, teased his fingers through the wispy little bits of a beard that clung to his chin like snot on a doorknob. He said something else to me. I stuck my nose in the air, remembered I wasn't supposed to make eye contact with men (sheesh! So many rules just to come to one country!) and tried walking away, but Mr. Wimpy Beard had my bag.

"Áram!" I yelled at him, trying desperately to remember the other phrases the Dig Egypt! people had listed in their program guide as useful Arabic. There was something about saying "stop touching me" that was supposed to be useful . . . oh, yeah. *"Sibnee le wadi!"* I yelled at the top of my lungs.

I guess they weren't expecting me to yell, because two of the four hissed at me and backed off, but the other two, including Beard Boy, just laughed and tried tugging my bag toward them.

"Illegitimate sons of a donkey," I snarled, which was Rob's suggestion of a good insult. They didn't seem to get that at all, and Mr. Laughy Pants just laughed even harder, jerking me and my bag forward until he had a hand on my wrist.

I looked around for a woman to help me, like both Mrs. Andrews—who had been to Egypt before with the school choir—and the Dig Egypt! people had recommended, but the women who were scurrying by all had bags of groceries, and no one seemed to be inclined to help me.

"Okay, I can do this," I told myself, trying to pull free from the Bearded Wonder. "*Áram, áram!* This is going to make—*áram* already!—for a really great story. No newspaper will be able to resist buying it. I will probably win the Pulitzaaaaiiiii! *Take your hands off my arm!*"

While I was struggling with the first guy, the second one slipped behind me and copped a back-of-the-arm grope. Which just wigged me out. And he pinched, too. Hard! I jerked my hand and bag away from the Beard Weenie, stomped on the foot of the second, and, deciding retreat was obviously called for, threw myself into the dark caverns of the nearest shop, racing around shelves and cases to the back, where I stood panting just a little and sweating a whole lot as I peered down an aisle of dusty sandstone statues toward the entrance.

The two guys stood in the doorway, obviously looking for me. I ducked behind a big fake mummy and watched as a little bent old man in a dusty blue caftan pushed aside a bead curtain and scuffed his way out into the shop. Behind him, pausing in the bead doorway, was another guy, a dark figure in a black muscle tee, black jeans, and a long ebony braid that hung down to his shoulder blades. The two touchy-feely guys said something to the old man, but he waved his hands in a shooing motion and must have told them to get lost. They didn't like that and started coming into the shop, but the guy in black stepped forward and said something that had them hesitating. After a couple of what I was sure were snarky comments, they left.

I used the sleeve of my tee to wipe the sweat off my forehead. (Don't make that face; I didn't have anything else!) Dragging my duffel bag by its handles, I carefully made my way down the aisle toward the old man, who was waving an ancient black feather duster over some objects on a shelf in a dark corner. The guy in black was up at the front of the store, bent over looking at a case near the doorway.

I'd had enough of the guys in Egypt already, so I kept my voice low when I approached the old man.

"Ahlan wa sah." The Dig Egypt! lit said it was polite to say hello and good-bye when you entered a shop.

The old man, humming softly to himself, gave a little jump and spun around clutching the feather duster. He squinted at me and raised his hand to his face like he was going to adjust his glasses, then made a *tch* noise when he realized he wasn't wearing them.

"Salam alekum," he responded, which I knew meant "peace be with you," a polite greeting. I also knew the correct response, thanks to Mrs. Andrews.

"*Wa alekum es sala.* Um . . . do you speak English? *Inta bititkalim?*"

"English, yes, yes, speak English much small, much small." The old man beamed at me. "*Insha'allah*, you speak slowly."

"Whew. No problem. I'm afraid my Arabic is pretty bad, but the Dig Egypt! people say that we should pick it up quick enough once we start hanging around the workers and stuff. My name is Jan, January James. I'm going to be working on an archaeological dig in the Valley of the Servitors. The tombs out near Luxor, you know? Anyhow, I'm here for a month to work on the dig. I'm going to be a journalist, and I thought this whole Egypt thing would give me a lot of things to break into the biz with."

"Tombs, yes, yes, tombs good. Eh . . ." The old man looked confused for a moment, rubbing the sharp ridge of his nose. "Valley of Servitors?"

"Yep, that's the place." I scooted my bag next to the small table that held an ancient cash register, well away from the guy in black who was still at the front of the shop, now squatting next to a box that apparently held a bunch of tools. I looked around, figuring I might as well get my shopping for Mom and the others out of the way while I waited for the gropers outside to get tired of hanging around. "So you sell, what, antiques and stuff?" I looked into a tray of beaded necklaces next to the cash register. "Jewelry is always a good gift choice. Everyone likes jewelry."

"Yes, yes, Valley of Servitors! You come here," the little old guy said in his dusty voice, pointing to the far corner with one knobby hand while waving me toward it with the other. "You come. Valley of Servitors."

"You have some replicas of stuff from the tombs? Like statues and jewelry and things like that? I know they've found a lot of things there in the last few years. Mom would probably like something like that because it's from the area I'll be working in." I put down a pretty pink-and-red beaded necklace and followed him to the back of the room, sneezing a couple of times at the dust his caftan stirred up as he hobbled down the aisle. There was one dim bare bulb in the middle of the small shop that didn't do much to shed light in the corners, which probably did a lot to explain the old guy's squint.

"Valley of Servitors," the man repeated, stopping in front of an old black bookcase. I looked. On the shelves was a pretty motley collection of items—a small brown stone sphinx that was missing a leg, a papier-mâché King Tut's golden mask, a couple of dingy blue scarabs, three amber-and-gold beaded necklaces hanging from a rickety wooden stand, and a dirty black bracelet stuffed behind them.

I fingered the beaded necklaces, trying to see how well they'd clean up. My mother liked amber; maybe a necklace would make a good gift from Egypt? "Um . . . how much are they?" I asked, pointing to the necklaces.

"How much, yes, how much. Valley of Servitors, how much. Yes."

I sighed, almost too tired to care. My T-shirt was glued to my back despite the fact that the sun had gone down. Little rivulets of sweat snaked down the back of my neck, slid down my spine, and joined their brethren captured in the waistband of my jeans. I was sweaty, lost, and had already yelled bad things at people my first hour in this country. Rifling through my mental files labeled Things I Had to Learn Before I Got on the Plane for Egypt, I trotted out the pertinent phrase for "how much is that?" *"Bikam da?"*

"Bi-kaem?" The old guy rattled off something.

I pulled out the letter from the Dig Egypt! people that had the hotel name and address, and a pen. "Can you write it down for me? I'm not very good at numbers yet."

He wrote down the number fifty. I looked it up on the list of currency conversions Rob had printed out for me before I left home. Fifty Egyptian piastres was a little more than eight dollars—well within my souvenir-buying budget—but Mrs. Andrews had told me how much fun she had bargaining with people in the stores, and said it was expected by the shopkeepers.

I grinned at the old man and crossed out the fifty and wrote ten.

His eyes lit up as he made a clicking sound with his tongue, tipped his head back, and raised his eyebrows. "Not enough! Not enough! Valley of Servitors. You see? *Rekhis.* Very cheap." He scratched out the ten and wrote forty.

À la Andrews, I tried to look like I was so shocked by his price I'd rather staple my fingers together than pay what he asked. "Too much! Too expensive. Let's try twenty." I wrote the number down below his.

He opened his eyes really wide and slapped his hand up against the side of his face, which I assumed meant he was ready to beat himself silly before he accepted that price. His gnarled, twisted fingers grabbed my pen and wrote thirty.

I pursed my lips and looked at the necklaces, fingering the little money I had changed at the Paris airport. Thirty piastres was about five bucks. "For all of them? All three? Oh, shoot, what's three; hang on, let me look it up . . . *talat! Talat* necklaces?"

He shook his head, saying, *"Wahid, wahid,"* as he scooped up the black bracelet and plopped it down in my hand, his elderly, arthritis-riddled fingers having no difficulty in quickly extracting the thirty piastres from the money I held in my hand.

I looked down at the ugly bracelet sitting on my palm. It was of some sort of black stone, with a small blue bird-shaped blob on the top. "Hey, wait a minute; my mother likes amber; I want the amber necklaces!"

"You take, very good. Valley of Servitors." He hobbled toward the front of the store, ignoring me as I followed slowly behind him, desperately thumbing through the Arabic phrasebook in hopes it had "I don't want this ugly bracelet, I want the three pretty amber necklaces, instead" as one of their translated phrases.

"Look . . . um . . . what's the word for old guy . . . ?"

I looked up from the phrase book just in time to avoid running into a tall black shape that said, *"Effendim."*

"What? Oh. Thanks. *Effendim,* sir, I want the neck-laces— Hey! Where'd he go?"

"In the back. Hassad is very old." The guy in black with the long hair turned to look at me. He was a little taller than me, and although he had dark hair and dark eyes like the guys outside, there was something different about him. For one, he obviously spoke English (with an accent, but it was a cool accent), and for another, he looked at me differently. The guys outside, even the older men, looked at me like I was a cherry on top of a sundae and they wanted to lick the whipped cream off, and how creepy is that? But this guy, he just looked at me like I was nothing different from any other girl. And he didn't stare at my boobs, which was a really nice change.

Until I thought about that.

Why wasn't he looking at my body? Was I that repulsive? Did he think I was too fat? Even guys who thought I was fat liked to look at my boobs, but not this guy. Oh, no, Mr. Sexy-as-sin with his long braid and his muscle tee and nummy brown eyes just looked at me like I was no more interesting than the ugly bracelet that was glued to my sweaty palm.

Sigh. Some days life just wasn't worth the trouble of chewing through the leather straps on the straitjacket.

GUY DISSES GIRL—SHE DIES DAYS LATER, ALONE, UNLOVED, LOST IN A STRANGE CITY OF WHIPPED—CREAM LICKERS

The cute guy in black was still staring at me as if he could barely stand to look at me, so I made an effort to drag my mind from the picture of me lying dead in a gutter, and thought instead about how nice it would be to see him staked out spread-eagled in the desert, naked, covered with orange marmalade and a thousand hungry ants.

I especially liked the naked part. "Hassad is old? You're kidding. So that white hair and doubled-up walk and knobby hands weren't just a clever Halloween disguise?"

"Is that supposed to be funny?" the guy asked. I changed the marmalade-eating ants to snapping turtles.

"It's called irony. Evidently you've never heard of it." I pocketed the bracelet and grabbed my bag as I gave a little mental shrug. The first guy I meet in Egypt who doesn't try to grab me, and he's a few walnuts short of banana bread. Just my luck. I started to sidle around his big black-clad hunkiness toward the door, planning on making my escape. Maybe the bracelet would clean up and Mom would like it even if it wasn't amber?

"I'm quite familiar with irony," the guy said in a stiff voice. "I'm also familiar with the fact that Americans think nothing of insulting elderly people. What you said was rude and discourteous."

Rude! Discourteous! Polite little old me? Piranhas! Now he was covered with marmalade—no, *gravy*—and piranhas. Yeah, I know, there are no piranhas in the desert. You have your fantasies, and I'll have mine.

I stopped and gave the guy a narrow, slitty-eyed look of utter scorn. "How can I be rude and discourteous to the old guy if he wasn't here to hear me say it? And what does being American have to do with anything?"

"I didn't say you were rude to him, I said you were being rude and discourteous. There is a difference. Or don't *you* understand irony?"

"Oh!" I dropped my bag and marched the three steps over to where Mr. Handsome stood looking all hot and droolworthy . . . and annoying as heck. I poked a finger into his chest. "Listen, buster, I'm all over irony! I'm the most ironic person you have ever met! I *am* irony! So put that in your water pipe and smoke it!"

"I don't smoke," he snarled.

"Yay, you!" I said, and decided that although this guy had obviously provoked (polite and totally courteous) me, I wouldn't lower myself to his level anymore. I lifted my chin, shot him a look that said the piranhas were accompanied by ravenous bears, and spun around to get my bag and leave.

"Typical American know-it-all," he said.

"Now, *that* I am not going to take!" I grabbed my

notebook from the duffel's side pocket and yanked the pencil from my jeans. "I want your name!"

He crossed his arms over his chest and tipped his head to the side in a move so smooth, he could have been the poster boy for Smug Incorporated. Even with all that smugness, I couldn't help but notice that he had some hieroglyphs tattooed on his left biceps . . . a very nice biceps. I had the worst urge to just run my fingers over it. . . . Eek! What was I thinking? Bad Jan!

"You want my name? You want me to marry you?" His gaze skimmed me from my dusty tennis shoes to my jeans, up to April's Big Apple tee, my chin, my lips (thinned in annoyance), finally ending at my hair. "Tempting as that is, I'm going to take a water check."

I blinked a couple of times. I do that when I need to think. I think it's the fanning process of my eyelashes that pushes more oxygen to my brain. "Water check?"

For the first time since he entered the room, his smug self-assuredness dropped a notch. Instead of feeling superior about his mistake, though, the self-consciousness that flashed in his eyes did something funny to my stomach. "That's not the right phrase?"

"Close. I think you mean rain check." His shoulders stiffened as he gave a sharp nod. I felt a brief pang of something, a little spurt of empathy that had me adding, "It's a weird phrase anyway. I mean, what exactly is a rain check? A check made up of raindrops? Too strange for words."

He didn't say anything, just looked at me.

"And as for the marrying comment, which was *so* off base, I just meant that I wanted to *know* your name, so I could include it in my scathing article about rude Egyptian guys who start leering and touching you the minute you walk off a bus."

"I've never been leered at when I get off a bus."

"Whoops, there goes my spleen; you're so funny I just laughed it right up and onto the floor. You're not a girl, Mr. Comedian."

"And you most definitely are," he answered, and for a second, just for a second, his eyes dipped to my boobs.

"I saw that! You stared at my chest!"

His eyes snapped up to meet mine. "I did not stare at your chest—"

"Yes, you did! I saw you!"

"I did not stare." His jaw tightened for a moment. "I might have looked quickly, but that was all."

"You're a boobmonger, pure and simple. Oh, don't give me that outraged look; I've met guys like you before." That wasn't strictly true, but hey, I didn't know this guy. I didn't have to tell him *everything*!

He was silent for another few seconds. "You are a very odd girl."

"And you're gorgeous and sexy and the most annoying guy I've ever met in my life, and I have five brothers, so I know an awful lot of annoying guys. Right, if you're not going to give me your name, I'll just make one up. How do you say 'boobaholic' in Arabic?"

He rolled his eyes.

I looked around the shop for inspiration, but didn't find anything in English. A glance out the doorway at a ragged, dirty yellow banner hanging by its torn corner across the street was a little more promising.

"Khan al-Khalili. That sounds smug and arrogant, like someone I could name." I made a note of the name,

19

stuck the notebook back into my duffel bag, and slung the bag over my shoulder.

"Khan al-Khalili is the name of the bazaar," the guy said. "My name is Seth Tousson, if you insist on knowing, and I was not staring at your . . . uh . . ."

"You're a dawg, pure and simple," I answered as I started toward the door, chin high in the air, trying to squelch the part of my mind that said I was just as bad as he was. While I might not have ogled him, I did think about running my fingers over his biceps. I suppose that qualifies as a quasi-ogle.

"A dog? You're calling me a dog?"

I turned back, biting my lip. Seth's voice sounded really angry, like I had said something horribly insulting. Everyone from Mom to Mrs. Andrews stressed how important it was that I be respectful and polite while in Egypt. I suppose calling someone a dawg wasn't technically respectful, but it wasn't that bad. I mean, let's face it, most guys are dawgs!

"I said you were a dawg. That's D-A-W-G, not dog."

He just stared at me like I had monkeys crawling out of my ears.

I waved my hand around like it would help me explain. "A dawg is . . . well, in this case it means a guy who likes girls. A lot. A flirty guy. A player, you know?"

"Player," he repeated, his dark eyes blank for a second, like he was thinking hard. "I know what a player is."

I was willing to bet he didn't, but figured if I told him what it meant, I'd be back in the land of rude and insulting, so I let it go. "Okay. You know, you speak really good English. Did you learn in school?"

"No," he said abruptly. "I'm not a dawg."

"Oh, then you don't like girls . . . oh. Sorry." Whoops! Could I put my foot any farther in my mouth? "I think I'd better be going."

"Wait," Seth said, his black eyebrows pulled together as he grabbed my arm.

I pretended that my mind wasn't going totally girly at the fact that he was touching me. Especially since he wasn't into girls.

"You said you were writing an article. . . . You are a reporter?"

I smiled at his puzzled look. "I am a journalist, yes. That is, I'm going to be one, just as soon as I sell a couple of my stories and the papers realize how good I am."

"And the story you plan to sell is about how rude you think Egyptians are?"

My chin lifted at the tone in his voice. It wasn't nice. "Think? I've probably got bruises on my arm from where I was grabbed! And that was just in the first five minutes! Yes, I'm going to write about how I was groped the second I got off the bus."

His gaze zipped down me again, this time quickly and without stopping on my boobs. "You are dressed inappropriately for a female. If you were harassed, it is your own fault."

"Oh!" I gasped. "Inappropriately? Me?"

"If you're going to visit another country, the least you can do is learn enough about it to be respectful of its culture," he snapped.

"I did learn about Egypt; that's why I'm wearing jeans instead of shorts, and I'm wearing the loosest top I have. Just how am I dressed inappropriately?"

"Your arms are uncovered," he answered. "And your

hair. Women here have both covered as a sign they are modest."

"Modest! Mrs. Andrews, the principal at my school, told me about her trips here. She says women are subjugated and don't have the same rights as the men, and aren't allowed to do a lot of things by themselves. That's not modest, Seth; that's . . . that's . . ." I dug around in my mind for one of the phrases that April tossed out during her "womyn's rights" phase. ". . . female oppression in a male-dominated patriarchal society frightened of feminine power!"

He looked a bit surprised by my words.

"What's wrong; sphinx got your tongue?" I asked sweetly.

"No, I'm too polite to say what I think, but since you asked, I'll tell you," Seth answered. "What you see as oppression, women in Egypt feel is a sign of social status and a rejection of Western culture in favor of their own."

Excellent! My first day in Egypt and already I was having deep, meaningful conversations about important social issues, the kind real journalists have all the time. All I needed was a few more of his comments, and the article would sell itself. I slapped an outraged expression on my face. "Oh, so you're an expert on what women feel?"

"No, I'm not an expert." He looked like he was grinding his teeth even while he spoke. "I'm simply pointing out that as is typical of Americans, your insensitivity to a culture other than your own blinds you to—"

"Insensitivity?" I interrupted him and gave him a really quality glare, the kind I usually save for my brothers. "Now I'm insensitive as well as immodest? Gee, thanks a lot. For a guy who admits he's not an expert on women, you're sure awfully full of opinions."

He *was* grinding his teeth; I could see it as a muscle in his jaw flexed. "I did not say you were immodest. I just explained to you why you were treated as you were."

"Right. So in other words, although you've accused me of bashing your country and your culture—which I haven't, other than pointing out that the men here seem to think nothing about invading someone's personal space big time—you're doing exactly the same thing by accusing me of being insensitive."

"You are impossible!" he said a low, hard voice, his eyes going all black and glittery.

"And you're a great big hairy, tyrannical, dominating dictator who wants to oppress me, which, I can tell you, is not going to happen in this or any other lifetime!"

His eyes widened as he stepped closer to me in a move that I was sure was supposed to intimidate me. *As if!* I took a step forward, too, so that the tips of my sneakers brushed against the toes of his boots. It was safe, after all. He wasn't likely to grab me like the other guys, not with him being gay and all. So I refused to give ground, lifting my chin until our noses almost touched.

"You have something to say to me, go ahead, say it. Take your best shot." I was so close I could see that his eyes weren't really black; they were a dark, velvety brown with little red and gold flares. I could also smell him—but it wasn't a bad smell. It was part spice, part leather. It was nice, actually, but I wasn't about to tell him that.

"Are you challenging me?" he asked, the thick, long

black lashes that framed his eyes making me a little bit jealous. Being a redhead, I had wimpy, red-brown eye-lashes that took tons of mascara to become visible with-out a microscope.

I shrugged. I wasn't quite sure what I was doing, other than enjoying standing really close to him, breathing in the spicy leather smell, admiring his eyes, and thinking again about running my fingers along the smooth, brown skin of his biceps. . . .

"*Ya rooh roohi*," he said softly, his breath fanning over my face. "*Ma fish Kahraba!*"

I would have made pouty lips at him, but standing as close as we were, I probably would have ended up kiss-ing him, and that was the very last thing on my mind. Not to mention his!

"That is so not fair. I'm not speaking to you in a lan-guage you don't understand."

"What sort of a person goes to another country with-out bothering to learn the language?"

"One who just found out four months ago she was going, and who had to pass all sorts of early exams just so she could spend a month working on an archaeologi-cal dig, and who didn't have time to learn Arabic on top of everything else. Besides, that's part of what I'm sup-posed to be learning during my month here. What did you say?"

He went still for a moment, his eyes narrowing. "You're working on a dig?"

"Yeah, a very important one, too. It's outside of Luxor, in a place called the Valley of the Servitors. I don't sup-pose you've heard of it. . . ."

He groaned and stepped backward a couple of feet, his eyes closed for a second. "I might have known. . . ."

"You might have known what? And what was that *ya roohi rooh* thing?"

"*Ma fish Kahraba*. It means there's no electricity there," he said, tapping the side of my head.

"No electricity . . . Oh! That's an insult! Well, you're not the brightest bulb in the pack either," I said in a huff, jerking the strap of my bag over my shoulder as I turned and stormed toward the door, pleased that I had stood up to him without calling him a poop as he deserved, or pointing out just how wrong he was about everything.

Everyone knows that tact is an important part of journalism.

"Like it's okay for him to judge people by whether or not they have their hair and arms covered, and then tell me I don't have any electricity in my brain! The rat!" I muttered to myself as I slipped outside after a quick scan for Beard Man and his sidekick. Neither was in sight, although the street seemed to have filled with even more people, donkeys, dogs, kids, cars, and lovely, wonderful smells that almost had me drooling. "All right, I'm calm. Even if *he* isn't respectful, I will be. This isn't my culture, so despite the fact that I think that parts of it are wrong—inappropriate, ha! No electricity, double ha with a side of slaw!—I will not make judgments. Journalists are always impartial. I am here to enjoy being immersed in another society and broaden my mind while experiencing a one-of-a-kind archaeological dig. . . . Oh, great. Now I'm even more lost."

I stood at a four-way intersection, buffeted by people

as they hurried by me, my senses overwhelmed again by the bright colors, the spicy smells of cooking food mingling with something much less pleasant (donkey poop), and the sheer volume of noise in the streets. Seth had called it a bazaar, which I knew was a really old marketplace, but this didn't seem so much like an ancient mall as it did an obstacle course. Not content to have stuff piled up in front of the open storefronts, all four streets were a positive minefield of objects pouring out of each shop: carpets, clothing, wooden statues, silver and gold vases and decorative objects, incense lamps, bags and purses, colorful furniture, baskets, spices, replicas of ancient treasures, bead and cloth curtains, herbs, henna paints, religious stuff like prayer beads, pictures made up of painted sand, mirrors. . . . I stopped trying to ID everything and clutched my bag tighter so I wouldn't inadvertently knock anything over with it.

"The question is, which way is it to the Luxor Hotel?" I gnawed on my lip as I looked for signs in English, but in the end I decided to follow my nose. I turned left and went down a street that had the most delicious odors of roasting meat wafting down it, teasing and tantalizing me until my stomach growled nonstop.

I was halfway down the street before I realized it had narrowed so much that cars couldn't even go down it, just people. The pathway was clogged with old ladies in galabiyyas (loose robes) and hijabs, old guys in their robes, and younger people in normal clothing, although I suppose what was normal for me wasn't necessarily normal for them.

I still got some stares from a couple of the guys as I did a sort of fish-spawning-upstream thing down the road, but at least no one decided to grab me again. My stomach chose that moment to growl and had me gazing longingly at the food cart where a pretty woman in a turquoise hijab was selling what looked like kebabs. "Walking. Walking is good. Walking is not fattening. Walking is healthy. Just make it back to the hotel, and then you can have dinner."

My stomach protested the thought, and I decided that although walking might be good for me, a taxi would be better. I came to another intersection and took a right, down a road that had few people on it. Fewer people meant more cars, and cars meant taxis, and taxis meant a ride to the hotel, where I would apologize to the Dig Egypt! person for being late, and tuck into a lovely, wonderful, lifesaving dinner.

"This has got to be the right way. Fewer shops, fewer people . . . um . . . hi!" Two men in jeans and white shirts loomed up in front of me. They were fair-skinned and blond, so I assumed they were tourists like me. "You wouldn't happen to speak English, would you?"

Blond number one (my height, short hair, goatee) looked at blond number two (taller, skinny, shoulder-length hair) before turning back to me. "Yes, we speak English."

He had a kind of singsong accent, like something Scandinavian, but it was perfectly understandable. "Oh, thank God. I'm trying to find the Luxor Hotel. Do you know which way it is?"

"It is this way." Blondie One pointed down a dark alley that was sandwiched between two rows of buildings.

"Really? Okay. Thanks." I started down the alley, nervously looking over my shoulder as the guys followed me. Yeah. I know what you're thinking: Brilliant move, Jan. A dark alley is *just* where you want to be with a couple of guys you don't know. Maybe they were staying at the same hotel? I stopped and turned back to them. "You're probably going to think this is really stupid, but my mother told me to never walk down a dark alley with guys I don't know. You wouldn't be some weirdo perverts who attack innocent American girls, would you?"

I was smiling when I said that, thinking they would laugh at the joke and assure me that no, they weren't perverts, they were simply optometrists/policemen/chiropractors who were lost, too, but damn if Blondie One didn't grab my arm and hiss, "Where is the handmaiden?"

"Where is the what?" I asked, really starting to panic as Blondie Two moved in front of me.

"The handmaiden. The old man said you have it. We want it. You will give it to us now."

"Oh, the handmaiden," I said, planning my escape. If I kneed Blondie One in the happy sacs, and nailed Blondie Two dead on the nose, I could probably get away.

"Give it to me now!" Blondie One hissed in a low, cruel tone. He jerked me toward him, which was his mistake. My brother August made sure that both April and I went to self-defense classes with him, and one of the first things they teach you is how to take your opponent off guard. Rather than pulling away from Blondie, as he expected, I threw myself toward him, jamming my knee in his crotch as hard as I could. I twisted away from him as he shrieked and doubled over, slamming my fist in Blondie Two's nose before racing in the opposite direction. Fifteen steps later I realized two things—first, I'd never outrun them, not with a duffel bag that weighed approximately the same as the entire population of the Solomon Islands, and second, dark alleys have a bad reputation for a reason.

The Blondie Twins had me pinned up against the dirty wall of one of the buildings before you could say *ma fish Kahraba.*

"I don't know a handmaiden, I swear!" I told the furious Scandinavian as he tightened his hand around my neck. Blondie Two said something in a language that I didn't understand.

"The old man said you took it," the first guy snarled. "You have not had time to get rid of it. You will give it to me now or Erik will take it from you."

I glanced over to the thug formerly known as Blondie Two, and swallowed. Hard. He was cracking his knuckles while giving me a slow, evil smile. He didn't look at all as if he were threatened by me, but I figured I had to try to intimidate them. Maybe if I sounded as tough as they did they'd leave me alone? There is a time and a place for lying through your teeth, and this was clearly it. "I told her to take off. Two streets back. I told the handmaiden to take a hike, so I don't know where she is. Okay? Buh-bye."

Erik said something to Blondie One, who narrowed his already icy blue gaze on me. I was willing to bet my entire year's supply of ChapStick it was not at all nice. Or polite. Or respectful.

"Now, this is where I'm going to start screaming for help," I warned Blondie as Erik came toward me, his evil grin making me sick to my stomach.

"Now we will search you," Blondie One said, his voice

making my skin crawl. "You may scream all you like. There is no one to help you."

I did scream then. I screamed for all I was worth when Blondie One walloped me. Hard. Right across the cheek. As if that weren't bad enough, my head slammed backward against the hard stone building, making me see stars for a second.

I slumped down the wall, blinking madly, feeling but not seeing hundreds of hands groping me, nausea swelling up in a wave of pure misery.

BIKER GANGS RUN RAMPANT IN MYSTERIOUS CAIRO BAZAAR!

A dull roar filled my ears as my stomach turned around a couple of times and decided it was going to empty what remained of lunch. I was just about to heave when the roar that I thought was blood in my ears stopped, and all of a sudden the hands searching my pockets were gone.

I lay there for a few seconds with my eyes closed, try-ing to convince my stomach that barfing wasn't really a good idea, when slowly, bit by bit, I became aware of the noise of guys yelling and grunting, accompanied by odd crashes and assorted *whump* sounds. I opened my eyes and stared in wonder as a man in black decked Erik. He slammed backward into the opposite wall, bounced twice, then fell flat on his face and didn't move. Blondie One was out cold, draped halfway over a box of garbage.

I looked back to the man in black, his eyes so filled with fury it made me shiver despite the heat. I looked at the motorcycle leaning up against the wall. I looked down at myself, more than a little surprised to find my arms and legs where I had left them.

"Wow. I mean, wow! That was awesome!" I said as Seth strolled over and stood glaring down at me. "You're, like, some sort of biker dude? That was so cool!"

"Why did I know it was going to be you causing all this trouble?" He shook his head as he reached down and grabbed my wrist, more or less hauling me to my feet. I wobbled a little when he let go of me.

"Steady," he said, holding on to my waist while I waited to see if my legs were going to agree to hold me up. "Did they hurt you?"

"That guy with the beard belted me." I wiped the dirt off my mouth while he gently touched my cheek.

"I'm sorry."

"Yeah, well, I'm sure according to you I had it coming, what with all my bare arms and hair showing and stuff, but they weren't Egyptian." I pushed myself away from him and looked around the alley for my duffel bag. It had been forgotten in the scuffle, but evidently a couple of guys had fallen over it during the fight, because one of the handles was torn, the zipper was busted, and some of my things were spread out on the ground.

"No, you didn't deserve that. No one deserves to be attacked. All I was trying to say earlier was that although Egypt is a progressive country, a lot of people here stick to the old ways."

Progressive? I could dispute that, but instead grabbed a handful of my underwear that was covered in dirt and shoe prints, and stuffed it into my bag. "Whatever. Thanks."

"Did they try to"—he paused for a second—"sexually assault you?"

"No. They thought I knew someone they were looking for. A maid."

"A maid?"

I took the hairbrush and pair of sandals that Seth had picked up, and crammed them into the bag along with a pair of jeans and two skirts that I had brought for times when I needed to dress up. "A handmaid. Thanks."

Seth held out my pair of tie-dyed tights that my sister April had made me for a birthday present, and the ugly bracelet the old man had shoved on me. The tights were torn and filthy, and for some reason just seeing their pretty pink and blue and purple colors all tattered and dirty in Seth's hand made me want to bawl.

"You're crying," he said as I took the torn tights.

"No, I'm not. I'm a journalist, and journalists don't cry," I said, wiping my dirty face with the tights. My throat ached with a lump of tears that I wanted to let loose, but there comes a time in every girl's life when she has to draw the line, and standing in a dark, dirty alley in Cairo with a sexy guy with long hair was where I drew it. I swallowed back the tears and wiped my nose on the tights.

"I don't think anyone will think less of you because you're crying," he said. "You're young to be a journalist. How old are you?"

"Sixteen. I'll be seventeen in three months." I sniffled back another lump of tears and hoped it was too dark for Seth to see that my face was all blotchy, the way it gets when I cry. "How old are you?"

"I'll be eighteen on Eid al-Fitr."

"Huh?"

"The end of Ramadan. It's a big feast. This year it falls on my birthday."

"Oh, Ramadan. I read about that starting a couple of days ago. We can't eat during the day, right?"

"Muslims fast, but it's not expected for visitors." He waved the bracelet at my duffel bag. "Here's your bracelet. Get your bag, and I'll take you to your hotel."

I started to reach for the bracelet, but just as I was about to take it a rat the size of a bulldog chose that moment to come thundering out from behind the wooden crates of garbage and head straight for me. I screamed, "Oh, my God, it's a rat!" and ran to hide behind Seth. He stomped the ground a couple of times, which scared the big ugly thing off.

I peeked around from behind him, and wouldn't let go of his back until he swore it was gone.

"Sorry to be such a big baby," I said as I released his shirt and prodded my duffel bag a couple of times with my toes to make sure it was rat-free. "It's just that I have this thing about rats. My brother used to keep them, and they were always getting out, and for some reason they liked to walk on me while I was asleep, and if you've ever woken up to find rats walking all over you, you'd be a bit weird about them, too."

Seth just gave me a look, and nodded toward my bag again.

"The zipper is broken," I said, and then the oddest thing happened. I don't know if it was the hassle with the guys, or the punch I'd taken, or the rat or the time difference or what, but suddenly I burst into tears. Over a zipper!

I couldn't see Seth well because it was getting really

dark, but the way he stood made me think he was uncomfortable. Oddly enough, it made me feel better. "You don't have any sisters, do you?"

"No." He waited a minute, then asked, "Why?"

I dug a small package of tissue out of my duffel bag and blew my nose so I didn't sound all snarfy. "When I was crying you didn't tell me to get a grip like my brother March would, or to stop sniveling, like August would have. You didn't even tell me I sound like I have a sock stuffed up my snot-locker, which is what Toby says."

"Toby?"

I wrapped my tights around the bag, tying it shut so my stuff wouldn't fall out of it. "It's short for October. He's my little brother."

He took my bag and hoisted it onto the back of the motorcycle seat. "Your brothers are all named after months?"

"Five of us are. The other five have normal names. My mom named them, but got tired of thinking up names by the time August came around, so my father named the rest of us. He wasn't very good remembering things, so he named us for the months we were born in."

He looked at me funny for a moment. "What's your name? April? May? June?"

"January. Jan for short. How come you're named Seth? It's not a very Egyptian name, is it?"

"More than you know," he muttered, swinging a leg over the bike, nodding his head toward me. "Are you coming or not?"

I looked at my bag sitting behind him.

"You'll have to hold it on your lap," he said, revving

the motor. I recognized the dull roar of it as the noise I'd heard just after Blondie belted me.

"Okay, but . . ." I looked over to where the two men still lay. Erik was moving, but Blondie was still out. "Shouldn't we do something about them? What if they're seriously hurt?"

"They aren't," Seth said, revving the motor again.

"How do you know?"

Even in the dark I could see him roll his eyes. "Because I didn't intend on hurting them seriously. Do you want a ride or not?"

I felt bad about leaving the two guys in the alley, but I'd feel worse about trying to find my way to the hotel in the darkness, so I pulled my bag up, slid my leg over the seat, and clutched the bag with one hand and Seth with the other as the bike moved forward. "What do you mean, you didn't intend on hurting them seriously?"

He said something, but I couldn't hear it with the noise of the traffic as we merged onto a busy street. At a stoplight I asked him again.

"Kyokushin karate," he said.

"Oh, cool, martial-arts stuff. So do you live here? In Cairo?"

He shook his head, which made his braid tickle my nose. The light changed just as I was going to ask him what he was doing in town, but I kept my mouth shut instead. Not only did I not want to distract him from driving (Cairo drivers didn't seem to believe that laws applied to them, and they pretty much drove however they wanted), I was also having problems with my hand. The hand that was holding on to Seth, that is. The other hand had the duffel bag, and that was no problem, but the Seth hand . . . somehow that had ended up clutching his stomach. Or rather, the T-shirt covering his stomach. I didn't want to let go of it, because what else was I supposed to hold on to? Down was *not* an option, while up meant his chest, and that was dipping into more *omigod* territory. I couldn't hold a guy's chest. That was just too . . . too . . . *intimate*. And besides, Seth probably wouldn't like me holding on to his chest.

A few minutes later we stopped at another light.

"If you pull over for a minute, I can get you the address to my hotel," I yelled in his ear (it was noisier now that we were approaching the downtown part of the city).

He shook his head again and yelled over his shoulder, "I know where the Luxor Hotel is."

I had to wait eight blocks before he stopped again. "How do you know which hotel I'm staying at? I didn't mention it."

"You're going to work at the dig in the Valley of the Servitors, aren't you?"

"Yeeees," I said slowly.

"That means you're staying at the Luxor. Stop squirming around. It's not too much farther."

I stopped trying to scoot myself back on the bike seat (I was smooshed right up against him, my thighs snuggling his, my chest pushed against his back). "Sorry. It's just that because of the motion of the bike, I'm plastered up against you, and since you're gay and all, I know you must not like my boobs being smooshed up against—"

He twisted around and gave me a look that should have scorched the hair right off my head. "I'm *what?*"

"Look, I said I was sorry! But there's not much I can do

about it, okay? I'm trying to keep back from you, but the stopping and starting makes me slide forward, and then there I am—"

"I am not gay," he interrupted me to say slowly, like he was having to chip the words out of granite.

I blinked a couple of times (obviously more oxygen was needed for my brain). "You're not? Then why did you say you were?"

"I never said I was gay."

"Yes, you did; you said it back at the shop. You said you weren't interested in girls."

"I said I wasn't a dawg! For your information, I like girls. A lot. It's just that they . . . Now what are you doing?"

I grunted a little tiny grunt as I hauled my bag up on one end so it acted as a barrier between me and Seth. "Arranging it so I won't be smooshed up against you."

"What?" A puzzled frown wrinkled his brow.

I lifted my chin and looked down my nose at him the way my mother does whenever someone criticizes her paintings. "It was one thing to be squished up against you when you were gay, but now that you're not, I couldn't possibly sit like that with you."

His pretty brown eyes narrowed for a minute before the car behind us started honking. He turned around and the bike jumped forward, but even with the noise of the traffic I heard him say, "You are the oddest girl I've ever met."

"I'm not odd, but I'm not a tramp, either. If you thought I was slut city before just because my arms and head aren't covered, you'd think I was a ho if I rode on a bike with you with my thighs touching yours and my arm around you and my face buried in your neck smelling your hair. Which . . . uh . . . I wasn't doing. But if I was, you'd think me immodest or something."

He said something, but it was lost in the traffic.

"What?" I yelled.

"I don't think you're immodest!" he bellowed back to me, turning his head to do so. The bike wobbled and sent both me and the bag sliding to the right.

I screamed and wrapped both hands around him, hugging the bag between us. I couldn't hear him, but I could feel his stomach move as he laughed.

Fortunately the hotel wasn't much farther. Another ten minutes and we rolled up outside the front steps of a big hotel. "Here you are," he said, both feet on the ground while I peeled myself off him, my legs a little shaky as I dragged both the bag and my body off the bike.

"Thank you; I appreciate the ride." I set the bag down and looked at him, wondering if I should offer to shake his hand. Mrs. Andrews said people in the Middle East were very big on handshakes, but maybe he expected me to kiss him? He did rescue me and then bring me to the hotel. Maybe I should kiss him? On the cheek or the lips? Would he think I was a tramp if I kissed him? Guys back home wouldn't—well, most of them wouldn't—but things were different here. Would he be insulted if I kissed him? Would he be sorry he rescued me if I didn't? Was a handshake okay if it was the girl who offered it?

"You know, this was a lot easier when you were gay," I said, holding out my hand. He looked at it for a minute, then started to shake it. I leaned forward and kissed his cheek. "Thank you for saving me. It was very nice of you to care."

His mouth hung open for a second, but before he

could say anything I grabbed my bag and ran up the stairs to the hotel lobby, blushing like mad.

January James, international sex goddess. Might look good as a byline!

"I'll say one thing about this whole Ramadan thing—you may have to fast during the day, but the food is definitely worth the wait!"

The girl to my left, Izumi Shikibu, giggled gracefully as she dipped a piece of 'aish shami (a puffy bread kind of like pita) into a bowl of delicious olive-and-pepper hummus that I'd commandeered. I stifled the urge to sink down into my seat, reminding myself that although Izumi might be pretty, and delicate, and skinny as a rail, and graceful and intelligent and everything else anyone could ever want—not to mention speaking English, French, and German in addition to her native Japanese— I shouldn't feel like a big old bloated carcass next to her. Comparisons were wrong. This wasn't a competition.

I was *so* in last place!

"Izumi, you try some of chicken tagine—wonderful it is being," Dag said. She reached the empty chair between us like I wasn't even there, and handed Izumi a small plate of stewed chicken and dates. "I know you will be being the appreciate of its flavors most complex."

I smiled at Dag and tried not to flinch when her steely gray eyes glared at me for a second. Dagmar Sorensson, Swedish so-called linguist and head of the student volunteers for the Dig Egypt! project, was not happy with me. Yeah, okay, so she might have some grounds for being a bit pissed at me, since I had missed the connection with her and the other Dig Egypt! students at the Cairo airport, and thus didn't get to ride back to the hotel with them, or visit the Cairo Museum with them, and she said she spent hours on the phone trying to find out what happened to me, but I did apologize. Three times. Once I even managed to rustle up a few tears. It didn't do me any good, however. When I had finally staggered into the hotel and asked for my room, the front desk called Dag, and she came down while I was handing over my passport and getting my room key.

An hour later she had finally wrapped up her lecture and warned me in her weird form of English that if I caused her any more problems, she'd send me home.

"Can she do that?" I had asked Izumi, my roomie, as Dag left, slamming the door behind her.

Izumi shrugged. "I think so. She seemed very angry."

"That's an understatement." I groaned as I collapsed on the bed. Two hours later I had managed to get a nap, take a quick bath in yellowish water that was evidently what they had in Cairo, and changed my clothes into the sage Godet skirt and matching ballet wrap top with teal butterflies that April designed as part of her "wearable artwork" exhibition. Sometimes hand-me-downs can be good.

By the time I made it downstairs for dinner, all the other high school students had gathered at a big round table in the middle of the room. Dag introduced me quickly, so quickly I didn't catch too many people's names, but it was pretty clear that almost everyone there was American. I slid into one of the two empty chairs next to Izumi. To her left was a girl named Kathy who seemed to be the group suck-up. Across the table was an Indian girl named Sunita, a French girl who apparently didn't speak English, a couple of other girls whom I didn't get to talk to, and a chatterbox named Chloe who seemed to be addicted to her lip gloss. I swear she put it on every ten minutes.

"Try pastilla," Dag had said after the intros were done and the food was being passed around. "Is very good for childrens."

"Sure," I said, scooping something in pastry onto my plate. I also added grilled chicken, *warak einab* (which is stuffed grape leaves and chicken livers), and a Turkish dish called *börek peynir*, which turned out to be cheese in a pastry, flavored with nutmeg, of all things. You wouldn't think nutmeggy cheese would be good, but after going what seemed like half a lifetime without food, I scarfed everything down, even the pastilla (it had cinnamon and sugar on the top, which is a weird thing to put on what was basically a spicy chicken pot pie). By the time I came to the *fattoush* (salad with the nummiest fried-pita croutons), I was stuffed. Which made me feel guiltier than ever as I sat there looking at all the other Dig Egypt! kids. I was sure that not a single one of them was on a diet.

Everything was peachy until a tall guy with a long black braid strolled over to the empty chair next to me like he owned the place.

I stared at Seth with my mouth hanging open for a second. "What are you doing here?" I finally managed to whisper. No one else was paying any attention to him, although he was so nummy-looking I couldn't imagine the girls weren't drooling on him. He had changed his clothes into regular jeans and a dark blue lightweight cotton shirt that was open halfway down his chest. He had a gold necklace with a cartouche hanging on it—one of those long ovals with hieroglyphics of a king's name in it.

He smiled and didn't even bother to lower his voice when he said, "Hello. I'm going to have a little kofta, if you'll pass it to me."

"You're going to get in trouble," I said, quickly looking around the table. Dag was lecturing Chloe about something she'd said, Izumi and Kathy were writing down each other's addresses, and the rest of the people at our table were in the middle of the restaurant learning how to do a belly dance.

"Eating kofta?" Seth tipped his head to the side and brightened his smile. My stomach did a full gainer with a half twist. "I don't think so. The sun has been down for more than two hours."

I passed him the plate of minced meat kebobs and frowned. He sure wasn't acting like himself. Before he was all dark and brooding and frowning and stuff. Now he was smiling. And just what was he doing here? "Look, Seth, I know I kissed you and everything, but that doesn't mean you can go all stalker on me. Surely even here they have rules about that."

He stopped stuffing his face with kebab to give me a slow grin. "You kissed me, did you? And you are . . . uh . . ."

"Jan," I hissed, wanting to pinch his arm. Hard. I looked away from him, swearing to myself over my stupidity. How could I have fallen for his "I'm not a dawg" line? He couldn't even remember my name a couple hours after he had saved me from the gropers! I blushed again thinking about how I had kissed him, wishing now

I hadn't, since he obviously didn't give a flying rat's pa-
tootie about me.

"Jan, that's right, how could I forget? So, Jan, would
you like me to show you around the area after dinner?
Maybe we could . . . talk . . . more." As he spoke, his
fingers caressed my hand, stroking up toward my arm.

"I don't think so." I moved my arm away so he wasn't
touching me anymore.

He smiled and waggled his fingers. Suddenly a watch
appeared in his hand, a familiar watch. I looked down at
my wrist, but it was bare. "Hey!"

"Little sleight of hand," he said, handing me back my
watch. I put it on, stiffening when I felt his hand on my
knee, sliding under the hem of my skirt. "If you think
that's amazing, you should see what I can do with just
one hand."

I clamped my hand down on his to keep it from going
beyond midthigh, pretending to be interested in the rest
of the Dig Egypt! people as they did a really awful belly
dance in the middle of the floor. "Oh, right, like I look
like I just fell off the stupid wagon? Think again, buster."

"Aw, Jan, don't be that way. I thought you liked me,"
he whispered in my ear. I stiffened as his fingers flexed
along my bare leg, wondering if anyone would notice if I
stabbed my fork into his hand. He must have taken a
bath, too, because he didn't smell like spicy leather anymore. Now he smelled like deodorant.

"Do you want to know what I like?" I asked, forcing
my lips into a smile as his fingers started to stray.

"Very much," he breathed.

I grabbed his fingers with both hands, bending his
thumb back to the point where I knew it was going to

44

start to hurt if I pressed any harder. His eyes widened when he realized what I was doing, but before he could say anything I leaned close to him and whispered, "I liked you better when you were gay. Go away and leave me alone. If you come near me again, I'm going to have Dag call the police. Got it? Good. 'Nighty-night, hope the bedbugs bite."

I slid out of my chair before he could protest, and headed out of the restaurant, intending to walk off some of the dinner I'd wolfed down.

"Where you are going now?" Dag followed me out to the hotel lobby. Rather than turning toward the stairs, I had crossed the lobby toward the front doors. "It is forbidden you should again wander. You make most big damage to reputation of Dig Egypt! program since earlier. I am not allowing damage repeating!"

"Look, I said that was a mistake, and that I'm sorry. I can't do anymore than that." I was a bit peeved with everyone. Seth, Dag, even tiny, petite, perfect Izumi were on my list at that moment. "I promise I won't go far. I promise I won't get lost. I promise I'll be ready to go first thing tomorrow morning."

"It is being unsafe for childrens to leave hotel at night," Dag said, folding her arms over her chest. She was a fairly small woman, but her voice was big. It was also harsh, with a heavy Swedish accent, and worked wonders on me whenever I wanted to giggle at her awful hair (orange, cut in an ear-length wedge that bobbed when she spoke). "Bad mens outside. Very bad. Childrens are not to be leaving hotel without chaperone."

I thought about just ignoring her, but my cheek still hurt where the big two-legged rat at the bazaar had hit me. I spun around, frustrated. I had to work off some of that dinner, or I'd look like a beached whale by the end of the month! "Right. Okay. No walking around outside. How about the garden? Seth . . . uh . . . someone said there was a garden. Is that allowed?"

She pursed her lips and shook her head, her orange wedge looking like she'd dipped her head in cheddar cheese and let it harden. "We are to be leaving at six in clock to be at dig in time for dinner. Now is not time for wandering. Now is time for childrens to be in bed sleeping sound sleeps."

I looked at the tiny clock over the registration table. "That leaves me an hour. I won't leave the garden, I swear. I just need to work off some of that dinner, okay?"

She eyed me in that way skinny people have. "You are being to eat too much. It is not healthy life."

I dug my nails into my palms and remembered that I had to be polite. Even to Dag. "Thanks for the advice. I'll try to remember it. I'll be in the garden if you want me."

"You will not be being anarchy! I am chaperone of childrens!" she yelled after me as I hurried to a side door I assumed opened to the garden. Her voice went up a couple of notches, going off the top of the shrill scale as she added, "You will be doing rules of conduct or you will be going home to Mama and Papa with note of behavior most bad!"

I ducked through the doors, sick to my stomach. How had everything gone so wrong in such a short amount of time? I'd gotten lost, but been rescued by Seth, who turned out to be a total jerk. Now I had Dag on my case threatening to send me home. Why did nothing ever go right for me?

I wandered down the veranda that ran around three sides of the hotel, did a bit of walking up and down the lush green garden, but eventually gave that up because the people sitting out there smoking and drinking wine and laughing and having fun were starting to stare. I ended up settling on a stone bench located at the far side of the veranda, just around the corner from the steps that led down into the garden. I curled up on the bench, screened by a squat, bushy palm plant, and gave in to a little wallow of homesickness, wishing for a few minutes that I were back home in the room that April and I shared, with Mom and Rob and everyone running around, and the dogs getting into trouble, and Mimsy, my cat, hacking up hairballs everywhere, and all the other stuff that was home.

Instead there I was, in a strange country where I'd been hit by one guy and kissed another who later groped my thigh, gotten yelled at by a woman who wanted to send me home, and had to share a room with a girl who was prettier and a gazillion times more popular than me.

"My life sucks," I told my feet. They looked like they agreed. I was just about to haul my sorry butt to bed and hope things would look better in the morning (they never did, but I didn't stop hoping they would), when I heard a familiar voice nearby. A voice whose owner I didn't want to see. I scrunched down lower behind the palm and carefully pulled aside a couple of fronds so I could see through it.

". . . no one around."

"I had to go to Magdi's shop anyway," Seth answered whoever was talking to him.

Great. Just what I needed. Mr. Octopus Hands right there, in the dark, just a few feet away from me. Silently I sank off the bench and hugged the wall. If he turned his head to the left he'd see me. I held my breath as the person hidden by the palm handed him a chunky manila envelope and said something in a voice too low for me to hear.

Seth shrugged and took the envelope. "Just for delivering a package? How much is it?"

I paused in the middle of slinking away. What on earth was Seth doing hanging around the dark end of the veranda, talking about mysterious packages and envelopes of money late at night when no one could see him?

No one but January James, wonder journalist!

"That's generous of you, but what will I say if my parents find it?"

Well, *that* sounded suspicious! Just exactly what was he involved in? Visions of me standing in front of a bunch of photographers, being handed the Pulitzer prize for investigative journalism (TEEN SINGLE-HANDEDLY UNCOVERS INTERNATIONAL DRUG/WHITE SLAVERY/SOMETHING ICKY PLOT!) clouded my vision for a moment. I hesitated between wanting to peek out and see who Seth was talking to, and escaping.

"Good idea. There's a Strat I have been wanting for a long time. Have you seen Jan? I thought she came this way."

The other person said something.

Seth laughed in response. "I don't think so at all. She's

just like a ripe fig waiting to be plucked, and you know how I love figs."

Ripe fig? Plucked? *Me?!* Well, that decided it. I sucked in my breath to make myself as skinny as possible, and slowly crept down to the dark end of the veranda, praying that he didn't see me.

Luck, for once, was with me. I had to jump over the edge of the stone railing to the ground, but the agony in my ankles from the four-foot drop was worth it to make my escape from Seth. The pain was much less by the time I hobbled around the hotel building. Just as I rounded the corner, I saw a familiar figure coming down the front steps. It was Blondie One. I couldn't see his face until he turned to wave at a cab. He slipped on a pair of dark glasses before he got into the cab, but not before I saw that his lip was cut and his eye was dark and swollen.

"Serves you right," I whispered, hiding by a spiky shrub until the cab left. I limped my way up the steps of the hotel and entered the lobby. Luckily it was empty— or it was until a dark-haired guy in black wandered out of the room that connected to the veranda.

"Jan," Seth said, his brows pulled together in a frown as he walked toward me. "Have you seen—"

"Fig plucker!" I yelled, and slapped him—right on the cheek I had kissed earlier. The beast. I spun around on my sore ankles and ran up the stairs to my room.

One day in Egypt and already my life was a mess.

MUMMY'S CURSE CAUSES FLATULENCE!

"And this will be your room, my dears. It's a bit small, but I'm sure you girls will make the best of it. Now, as I said earlier, we all eat lunch on site with the rest of the dig crew, but you're to take your breakfast and dinner here at the monastery. Abdullah is an excellent chef, so I'm sure you will enjoy the cuisine here. I told Dr. Tousson many years ago that being on a dig was no excuse to be uncivilized, and I stand by that." The woman who'd introduced herself as Kay fluttered around the room, opening the wooden shutters on three small glassless windows. She was American, had a short dark blond bob, wore a taupe-and-lavender linen pantsuit, and the way she fussed with the covers on the bed and the chairs made me mentally dub her the Martha Stewart of the desert.

"Tousson?" I asked as I dumped my dirty, torn, held-together-by-tights duffel bag onto one of the two small beds that were crammed into the tiny room in an old abandoned monastery, sliding a glance at Izumi to see if she minded me claiming the bed. She was bouncing on the other one, apparently happy.

"Yes." Kay turned to smile at me, one of those big

toothy smiles adults always use with teens. "Oh, didn't I introduce myself properly? I'm Kay Tousson, and my husband is Dr. Reshef Tousson. You know all about him, I'm sure. Anyway, as I was saying, I'm delighted to have you both on the conservation team. Normally we wouldn't accept student helpers for such delicate work as the conservation of the tomb walls, but what with Maria and Benedict off on their honeymoon for a month, it seemed ideal to have you fill in for them, especially since you have such an artistic background, Jan. Imagine having the daughter of two such famous artists as Renata and Brendan James on my conservation team!"

I flinched. The last thing I wanted to do was be assigned any work having to do with arty stuff. I'd tell her later, once we were alone, that I was the only member of my family who couldn't draw, paint, design, or sculpt anything. Right now I had something else on my mind. "You . . . uh . . . wouldn't happen to know a guy named Seth Tousson, would you?"

Her smile faded a little. "Do I know . . . Didn't you meet Seth on the trip out from Cairo?"

I looked at Izumi. Her mini alarm clock had failed earlier that morning, leaving us both oversleeping and subsequently in a mad scramble to get to one of the three vans that was arranged to take the Dig Egypt! students to Luxor. By the time Izumi and I ran down the stairs to the front lobby, it was twenty after six, and Dag, pacing in front of the last van that had been held up for us, read us the riot act the whole way to Luxor.

Well, not the whole way. It's a ten-hour trip, and she spent a good part of it lecturing Izumi, me, and the French girl who didn't speak English about how we weren't to touch any of the objects found on the site, since they were all cursed.

"Cursed?" I had asked, thinking that would make for a great article subject. "You mean cursed as in, curse of the mummy cursed? Ugly bald guy with bad teeth, trailing bits of brown wrappings, chasing girls down long, dark hallways cursed?"

Dag shot me a look that by rights probably should have dropped me dead on the spot. Talk about cursed! "An attitude such skeptical is not fine. Curses are very bad for childrens. They scare most horribly pipples of Egypt. Not to be taking curse of mummies dead Tekhen and Tekhnet lightly! Curse has killed much worse than pipples!"

"What could be worse than death?" I whispered to Izumi.

"Ten hours in a van with Dag?" she whispered back.

I laughed so hard I snorted, which brought Dag's attention back to me, something I had realized was not a good idea. Just remembering it as I stood in the stifling heat of the monastery brought little shivers of unpleasantness. Although the ride down with Dag had been a nightmare, it was a nightmare that hadn't included Seth.

Until now.

"Um . . . no. Seth wasn't on the van. Is he connected to the dig?"

She gave me an odd look. "Seth is my son."

My jaw dropped.

"My youngest son, actually. Youngest by four minutes. His twin, Cy, is the oldest. You didn't meet him either? I'm sure Seth rode his motorcycle to Cairo, since he takes that horrible thing everywhere—it's a mother's worst nightmare, him riding around without a helmet, and with the state of the roads in Egypt—but I'm surprised you didn't see Cy. They were both in Cairo, although you know how boys are—always off doing their own thing. Still, Cy makes a point of meeting all the new students. He does enjoy meeting the young women. He's a good boy, but . . . well, I needn't tell you what it's like to be young."

"Twins?" I croaked, absolutely horrified. The vision of Seth danced before my eyes . . . a dark, brooding Seth in the shop, the dark, menacing Seth in the alley as he karate-chopped the gropers, the suddenly smiling, thigh-touching Seth at dinner, and later, a smug, fig-plucking Seth . . . oy. Two Seths. Twins. Seth and a Seth-substitute. And I'd slapped one, and almost broken the thumb of the other. Both sons of the archaeological dig head and his wife, my bosses for the next month. "Identical twins?"

"Oh, yes, very much so. The only way to tell them apart is Seth's horrible tattoo."

"Man, I am such an idiot," I moaned, sinking down onto the bed.

"I'm sure it's not as bad as all that," Kay said in that chirpy, happy tone adults get when they see teens self-destruct. "I know you're sorry you missed them in Cairo, but you'll meet them now that you're here. I'll introduce you, if you'd like. I'm sure the boys will be as thrilled as I am to have Brendan James's daughter here."

She beamed at me for another moment, then said something about washing up for dinner, pausing at the door to add, "I should warn you girls that technically we're on a water ration, since the monastery well is shared with the workers at the dig, but what they don't know can't hurt them, now, can it? Just don't use too much water in your baths, all right?"

I groaned and fell back on the hard, lumpy bed as Kay drifted out the door, saying something about having to tell all her friends just which famous artist's daughter was on her conservation team.

"Your father is a famous artist?" Izumi asked as I covered my face with a wimpy pillow, trying to erase from my mind the mental image of the shocked look on Seth's face when I slapped him.

I peeked out from under the pillow. She was carefully unpacking her two bags, placing the neatly folded clothing into the wooden chest at the foot of her bed. Even after a ten-hour van ride, she looked perfect. She wasn't sweaty, rumpled, or sunburned, as I was. I tried hard to hate her, but she was just too nice to hate.

Which was yet another form of perfection.

"Actually, my whole family is pretty famous. My mother and father were noted muralists until my dad died, and now Mom has turned to mosaics. My brother Alec creates environmental paintings—stuff like dressing up trees in an endangered forest, and bringing the press in to take pictures. My brother August is a sculptor. He's in Italy studying on a scholarship. My sisters Denise and April design fabrics, batiks and things like that. My sister Kara makes tapestries. My oldest brother, Nash, has his own line of comic books, and Alexa—she's another sister—is in Japan working for an anime company. My younger brother Toby is heavily into digital graphics— Digimon rules his life—and March is a book illustrator."

Izumi paused in the middle of tucking away lacy undies, her eyes big. "How many brothers and sisters do you have?"

"Nine. I'm the ninth of ten. How many do you have?"

"None," she said, looking at me as if I were some sort of giant insect lying on the bed. "Your whole family are artists? That must be wonderful."

"Yeah, right," I said, rolling onto my back and covering my face with the pillow again. "It's so wonderful I couldn't wait to get out of there. Do you have any idea what it's like to belong to a family where everyone is talented except you? I'm the only one in the family who can't do anything. I can't paint, can't draw, can't sing, dance, or play a musical instrument, school is just a way to pass the time, and I don't have any hobbies other than pretending I can actually do something. I'm a freak. I'm just a freak, that's all."

Izumi laughed. She even did that perfectly, in a nice, cheerful, amused way that wasn't at all offensive. "Oh, Jan, I do like you. If you're a freak then so am I, because I can't do any of what you said, either. And you have a talent—you're smart!—otherwise you wouldn't be here on the dig. Only the smartest students were accepted into the program."

"Or those whose stepfather serves on the board," I muttered darkly. I tossed the pillow aside and sat up, figuring I'd better put my stuff away, too. "There is something I'm hoping to do, though, and that's part of why I wanted to come here. I'm going to be a journalist."

Izumi looked up from where she was setting a bag full of bath things on a small dresser next to the bed. "A journalist?"

I scooted down to the end of the bed and dragged my bag over, unwinding the tights so I could dump the things into the chest at the end of my bed. "Yeah, the kind who write those great stories in the trashloids you see at the grocery store."

"Trashloid?" she asked, her head tipped to the side. She had long, black hair that made my little redheaded heart green with envy.

"Trashloid means tabloid. 'Monkey Boy Marries Dog Girl'—that kind of tabloid. They're really fun. Anyway, I read somewhere that the people who write those stories make a ton of money, and I figured how hard can it be to write up stuff like that? So when Rob—he's my step-dad—asked if I'd like to go to Egypt for a month to work on this dig, I figured this would be a great chance to work up a few good stories that I could sell to the tabloids. Mummy's curse and all that stuff."

Izumi grimaced. "Then you should be talking more to Dag. She seems to have the curse on her head."

I did a few therapeutic blinks. "Her head?"

Izumi patted her hair. "Yes, it's all she thinks about."

"Oh, on her brain. Yeah, you're right about that."

Her gaze dropped like she was ashamed of some-thing. "I'm sorry, my English isn't very good yet."

"Are you kidding?" I gawked; I positively gawked at her. "Your English is better than mine! And you speak other languages as well. That's *another* thing I can't do."

I would have thrown myself into a really quality pity party, but Izumi just laughed again and trotted off to take a tour of the grounds. Since it was at least a thou-sand degrees outside—and only nine hundred inside—I spent the next hour dumping my things into the chest and wandering through the abandoned monastery peeking into various rooms. The building itself was pretty slick—two levels of beige stone, shaped like a big square, but totally open in the middle to a courtyard where a couple of dusty trees shaded a cluster of tables.

The bedrooms were on the second floor, and steps led up to the flat roof, where Kay said a lot of people slept at night because it was cooler.

"What if you fall off while you're asleep?" I asked that night at dinner.

"Then you would break yourself," Dr. Paolo, the head conservator, said without looking up from the notepad he seemed always to have with him. He was Italian, an old guy with thick round glasses that magnified his eyes so he looked bug-eyed. I was starting to get the feeling that although Kay was officially the leader of the conservators, it was Dr. Paolo who really knew what he was doing.

"Think I'll pass on the roof-sleeping," I said, and concentrated on eating the cucumber salad and only a tiny bit of the chicken-and-rice dish that smelled like heaven, but which I knew wasn't going to be in the least bit diet-like. Because there were four Egyptians on the conservation crew, three of whom were Muslims—Sayed (nice guy with a birthmark on his face), Ahmed (snob who didn't look happy to see Izumi and me sit down to dinner), and Gemal (seemed nice, but was very quiet)—Kay explained that we'd be following Ramadan mealtimes, which meant we could eat dinner only after the sun was down, and have breakfast before sunrise.

"Of course, it's up to you girls whether or not you wish to partake of lunch with the rest of the dig crew. You're certainly welcome to—no one here will think any less of you if you do not wish to honor Ramadan."

Izumi and I glanced at each other, then around the table. Ahmed frowned at us, Sayed smiled, and Gemal kept his eyes lowered.

"Mind you, I think it's an excellent opportunity to explore and celebrate another culture by participating in the religious events," Kay said, taking another piece of the soft flatbread that made my mouth water just looking at it. "I wouldn't think of insulting my Egyptian brothers and sisters by not following tradition, but that's just me."

I was just opening my mouth to say that I would be happy to fast during the day as well—a big fat lie, but hey, when in Rome and all that stuff—when the big wooden door that separated the courtyard from the outside swung open, and Seth walked in. At least I thought it was Seth. If he and his twin were identical, which they certainly seemed to be from what I saw, then it could be the other one. . . .

"There you are!" Kay chirped, waving him forward. "Seth, have you met Izumi and Jan? Where have you been all this time? I expected you earlier."

My face went red as Seth gave me a long look before taking the empty seat across the table. "I was working on my bike, and then I heard Hussein had a find while sifting dirt from the burial chamber, so I went to look at that."

Kay gave a delicate shudder. "Darling, it's bad enough one son has gone over to the other side; I won't have you grubbing around like a common digger."

"Dad started as a digger," Seth said, his frown turning into a scowl. "I don't see why Cy is allowed to dig and I'm not."

"Your father was *never* a common digger," Kay said firmly, her smile going a little tight. "He was apprenticed to one of the greatest Egyptologists of the time, a man who recognized your father's superior intellect and abilities. As for Cy, I've explained to you several times that your father and I agreed that one of you would work with him, and one with me. And really, darling, you must admit that it's far nicer work to be conserving those lovely walls rather than rooting around in the dirt like an animal."

"I don't like conservation. I want to dig like Dad," Seth growled.

Kay laughed as she turned to the rest of us. "Just like his father, always snaps when he's hungry. Have some hummus and chicken, darling. You'll feel better after you've eaten."

I thought he was going to explode at that, and given the way his mother's eyes widened as he snarled something under his breath, I think she might have thought so, too. Instead he just slammed back in his chair and stormed off to the stairs to the upper level.

Michael, the fourth Egyptian conservationist (and a Copt, which meant he was Christian instead of Muslim), crossed himself as Seth leaped up the stairs. Paolo pursed his lips and went back to making notes with one hand while he fed himself with the other. Sayed, Gemal, and Ahmed kept their gaze firmly on their plates, although I thought I heard Gemal mutter, "*masha'allah*," which I knew was asking Allah for a blessing. Izumi also avoided looking at anyone in particular. I glanced away from Kay, who tried to laugh off Seth's hissy fit, even though I could tell she was embarrassed.

"Boys! I'd much rather have had girls. They're so much easier to handle," she said smoothly, and changed the subject to explain to Izumi and me just what the conservation techniques consisted of.

I listened with half an ear while Kay explained that the damage to the tomb was caused by a combination of water and corrosion within the tomb itself, all the while feeling bad because I'd slapped Seth by mistake, and also because his mom was one of *those* mothers, the kind who don't listen at all.

"And so what will we be doing?" Izumi asked as I tried to think of what I was going to say to Seth. I had to apologize for slapping him, but if I explained that I thought he was his brother, then he'd want to know what Cy did that made me want to slap him, and I don't think I could possibly explain about the thigh grab and the fig comment without dying of embarrassment.

"You will work with Sayed cleaning the paintings in room G. Last year we consolidated the paint with an acrylic solution, and reattached missing plaster, and this year our task is to clean the walls."

Then again, if I didn't tell him why I smacked him, he'd think I'd gone totally Springer or something, and he'd want to stay away from me because I was obviously psycho.

"So our job will be to fix the paintings?" Izumi asked. "Make them whole again?"

"No," Paolo said quickly. "Our job is to stabilize, consolidate, and clean. That is all. We do not restore, just conserve."

Which would be worse, I mused as I allowed myself just one more piece of garlic-dusted pita, to have him think I was an idiot for not realizing he was a twin—which really was not my fault, since he never mentioned he had a brother—or to have him think I'd kiss him one minute and slap him the next?

I sighed as I chewed the warm pita. Why was life so hard?

"I understand. I look forward to cleaning the paint-ings," Izumi said graciously.

Or more specifically, why was *my* life so hard?

"I thought since Jan is an artist, she can do the ren-dering of the walls into watercolor."

I stopped in midchew to stare at Kay, swallowing a big lump of pita to stammer, "What? Me? Watercolor? Huh-uh!"

"Don't be modest; you're ideal for the job."

"Um . . . no, I really don't think it would be a good idea."

Kay set down her fork and cocked a perfectly arched brow. "Not a good idea? Why?"

Think fast, brain. Anything but the truth ("I suck at painting!") would do. "Er . . . watercolor isn't really my medium. And you know how we artists are—we stick to our media."

That wasn't strictly the truth, but I was hoping that Kay was like my mother's pseudo-arty friends, people who pretended they understood the mind of an artist, but really didn't have a clue.

"Oh, yes, of course, we couldn't expect you to work out of your medium," Kay said quickly, just like Mom's friends did. "Er . . . what exactly is your medium, dear?"

Whoops, back to think-fast time. I ran my mind over all the possible art-form media that would be totally un-suitable to reproducing ancient Egyptian paintings.

"Leaf mold," I answered, remembering something that April had tried once. "I use leaf mold to make sculptures."

Kay's face went blank. As a matter of fact, so did

everyone else's faces. Even Izumi looked at me as if I were speaking gibberish.

"You use *leaf mold* to sculpt?" Kay asked, her voice incredulous.

I settled back in my chair, smiling at the look of confusion in her eyes. "Lots and lots of leaf mold, as a matter of fact. But not just any leaf mold; it has to be special leaf mold. From . . . um . . . frilly-edged willow trees. That's the best kind of leaf mold. Do you happen to know if there is a big supply of frilly-edged willow leaf mold in the area? Because if there's not, I couldn't possibly reproduce the paintings. It would . . . uh . . ." I dredged up the excuse that one of my sisters frequently used to get out of doing the laundry. "It would hamper my muse."

"Oh, dear, we couldn't have that." Kay looked concerned for a moment, her blue eyes disappointed as she gazed at me.

It was a look I was sadly familiar with.

"I have an idea," I said, pretending I'd just thought of it. "Why don't Izumi and I switch jobs? I could do the cleaning stuff, and she could paint the walls."

Kay looked from me to Izumi, her brow furrowed. "I don't suppose you have any talent at watercolor? It's not vital that we have a painting of the walls, of course, since the entire phase of conservation is being documented via photography and videotape, but it is traditional to have a member of the team duplicate the walls for archival purposes."

"I would be happy to try," Izumi said modestly, and for a few seconds I gave in to the pang of jealousy that hit me when Kay beamed at her.

No one ever beams at me, grouchy inner Jan complained.

Just wait until I start selling stories, I told her. *Then they'll all stop thinking I'm such a loser.*

"I'm sure you'll do fine, although . . ." Kay gave me a sad little look that had me squirming in my chair. "Well, it's no use bemoaning what can't be. We'll simply have to make the best of the situation. Jan, you'll work with Sayed and Seth. Izumi, I'll show you where the art things are after dinner, and explain to you which walls to paint first, all right?"

Seth? I had to work with Seth, too? Not just see him, but work with him? I toyed for a second with the thought of saying I'd paint the stupid walls, but the knowledge of just what Kay would think if she found out I was talentless, kept my mouth shut.

By the time dinner ended, I'd come to two conclusions: First, if I had to work with Seth, then I'd prefer to have him not thinking I was a total ditz, which meant I had to go find him and apologize for slapping him and calling him a fig plucker, and second, I was never going to kiss a boy again. It just ended up causing more trouble than it was worth.

"Get it over with, Jan," I said on a sigh as the others toddled away after dinner.

Before Abdullah the cook could come out with his helpers to clear the table, I grabbed a cloth napkin and filled it with pita bread and bits of grilled chicken, all topped with a carefully balanced cup filled with lentil soup.

"Where did Jan go?" I heard Kay ask Izumi from the

long room that ran the length of the house. "I wanted to show her some of my sketches and see what she thinks."

"She said she wanted to take a walk," Izumi answered as I crept by one of the doors to the room, hurrying to the stairs. "I will look for her if you would like."

"No, I don't think we should bother her if she's out consulting her muse. Those artistic types are temperamental, you know."

I stifled a snicker as I ran up the stairs to the second floor. I hated to lead Kay on by making her think I was as artsy-fartsy as the rest of my family, but if it would keep her off my back for a bit while I apologized to Seth, then I'd live with the lie. I checked all the rooms on the second floor, but didn't see him, which meant . . .

"I just hope I don't fall off the edge," I muttered as I climbed the dark, narrow stairs that led to the roof. "I'm going to be so pissed if I die before I sell a story."

There was a lovely soft breeze on the roof, a scented breeze that lifted the smell of the flowers grown in small pots in the courtyard, mingling with the smell of wood smoke and something warm and slightly acidic that I had decided was just the smell of Egypt. The soft glow of the oil lamps below didn't penetrate the darkness above, but there was enough of a moon to let me see the landscape of the roof. It was totally flat except for two short, squat chimneys on either end of one side of the monastery. I wandered toward the nearest, the shadows beyond it blacker than anything I've seen. I felt my way through the inky denseness, but no one was there. The sound of laughter and conversation drifted upward from the sitting room, but it seemed far away and unreal, as if it were just another background noise like the cicadas that chirped all night long, or the distant sound of night birds crying high above me.

Keeping well clear of the edge of the roof, I made my way over to the second chimney stack, and just about dropped the food when a voice rumbled out of the darkness concealed behind it. "What are you doing here?"

"Jeezumcrow!" I jumped, my heart beating madly even though I had hoped Seth would be there. A dark shape separated itself from the chimney. "Man, just give me a heart attack, will you?"

"What are you doing here?" he repeated, stepping forward so the little bit of moonlight slanted down on him. He didn't look happy to see me.

I swallowed hard, trying to remember what I was going to say in apology. My mind went blank, but luckily I remembered the food in my hands. I shoved the napkin of food and cup of soup toward him. "I brought you dinner, since you missed yours."

He looked down at the food, then up at me. "Why?"

I just knew he was going to ask that. Pooh. "Um . . . just because. I know you must be hungry if you've been fasting all day. You are hungry, aren't you?"

He shrugged and walked over to the edge of the roof, not seeming to be concerned in the least by the fact that there was nothing there to keep him from falling over the edge.

"I'll just put it down here, okay? If you get hungry, you can eat it. If you don't want it . . ." It was my turn to shrug, not that he saw, since he was looking out into the night. "Whatever. Night."

I took five steps before he spoke. "What did Cy do to you?"

"How do you know he did something to me?" I asked, looking back toward him.

He turned to face me, but he was in shadow, so I couldn't see his expression. Just the top of his head was highlighted by the moonlight, making it look like his black hair was tipped with silver. "The only time girls slap me is if they think I'm my brother. I'm always blamed for what he does. So what did he do this time?"

I thought about telling him, but suddenly it didn't seem important. What mattered was the thin edge of pain in Seth's voice. I knew that pain—I'd felt it often enough. A little feeling of warmth blossomed to life in my stomach. "I'm always getting blamed for stuff my brothers and sisters do, too. It's not fair that I should be punished just because—" I stopped. There was no need to tell him I was the talentless black sheep of the family.

"Because what?"

I made a face that I doubted he could see. "Doesn't matter. I know what it's like to be blamed for stuff you didn't do, though, and I'm really sorry I slapped you. I didn't know you had a brother. He's not very nice, is he?"

Seth froze. "Are you kidding with me?"

"Kidding me. There's no *with.*"

He froze even more until I said, "Look, English is hard enough even when you're born to it, but if you don't want me correcting you, I won't. I'm not trying to be a know-it-all or anything. I just thought that you'd want to know how to say stuff right."

"I do," he said stiffly. "Thank you."

"No prob," I answered. "And no, I'm not kidding you. Any guy who purposely lets a girl think he's his twin is a poop. You know what a poop is, right?"

He made a little waving gesture with his hand, like he was brushing away the question.

"It means a jerk. A spazzo. A dill weed. Someone not nice. I hope you don't mind me calling him that, but it's what I think he is. So I'm sorry I slapped you, and I'm sorry your mom was ragging on you in front of everyone, and I hope you eat the food because the chicken is really good, and I'll go now so you can be by yourself. I know how nice it is to be by yourself when everyone is picking on you. You don't have to worry that I'll tell anyone where you are, in case they ask."

I made it to the stairs before he spoke again, and even after the words drifted away on the soft evening breeze, I still wasn't sure I'd heard them correctly.

"They think I'm the reincarnation of an evil god. No one will ask you where I am. No one cares."

MYSTERIOUS TIME WARP IN EGYPTIAN TOMB MAKES DAYS FIVE TIMES LONGER THAN NORMAL!

The next two days were kind of a blur. A couple of high points stand out in my mind, like walking back to my room wondering how anyone could believe Seth was evil, reincarnated or not. I'd known him for only a day, but even I could see he was only bad—the *baaaad* kind of bad, not evil. I thought of asking Seth what he meant by his cryptic statement, but he had turned his back on me again, so I ended up going down to my room without finding out what he was talking about. When Izumi came in later I borrowed her book of Egyptian myths, figuring I'd read up on the bad gods to see if I could pick out the one Seth was supposed to be.

I didn't have time to read it, though. In order to eat breakfast, we had to wake up before the sun rose, and we had to scarf down enough food and water to keep us going until sundown. That was the theory, anyway, but our first day on the job both Izumi and I were so melted by the heat of working in the tomb, we stumbled after the other non-Muslim dig workers to the big mess tent.

"I shouldn't do this; I shouldn't do this. I said I was going to honor Ramadan, and here I am, caving in on my first day." I followed Izumi up the steep, rocky incline that led to the plateau where the dig employees lived. The big sand-colored mess tent was in the middle of the cluster of smaller tents, edged with a couple of trailers that held the more valuable dig tools and artifacts. Sweat rolled down my back under the white T-shirt and white cotton pants we were required to wear when we were in the part of the tomb that was undergoing conservation. "I should grit my loins and gird my teeth and suffer through it. I'm just a great big old wimp, that's what I am. It's just a little food and water, after all."

"This is our first day. I don't think anyone will think you are a wimp for wanting to eat, and if you don't drink, you could have the heat exhaustion. It is very hot in that tomb!"

"Hellish is more like it." I panted as I paused at the top of the climb to yank up the straw hat Kay had insisted I wear out in the sun, and mopped my forehead with the hem of my T-shirt. "You'd think they could get a couple of fans or an air conditioner or something in there, but noooo, we have to melt just to keep the precious walls happy."

Izumi giggled and tugged me toward the tent. "You are so funny when you complain. But look, here is everyone coming to lunch. You will be just like everyone else having lunch."

"All the infidels, yeah, but Kay said it would be a

good experience to go native, and I want to; I really want to."

"No one will think anything bad about you eating," Izumi reassured me, waving and calling out to a couple of the other Dig Egypt! kids who were dragging themselves toward the mess tent. She ran off to talk to them (without a single bead of sweat showing anywhere on her, while I looked like the Amazing Melting Girl). I stumbled toward the tent, pausing for a moment as I passed Dag arguing with the dark-haired girl named Chloe. She was shaking a tube of lip gloss at Dag.

"What do you mean there's no more water? That's stupid; of course there has to be more water!"

Dag frowned at Chloe. "Childrens yelling at chaperone most good is not allowed. You are water whore. Wasting water there and here as if no tomorrow is coming!"

I snorted. Water whore?

Dag stopped speaking and transferred her frown to me. Chloe smiled and dabbed on a bit more lip gloss. The kind with sparkles in it. Just the sight of her shiny, glossy, sparkly lips had me gnawing on the tendrils of dried skin that clung to my own lips, leaving me wondering if I had remembered to put my ChapStick in the backpack that I'd left in the volunteers' tent.

"*Ja?*" Dag asked in a snappish tone. "You are wanting what from me?"

I tried to smile under the effect of her glare, but it wasn't easy. "Hi. I just wondered if either of you has seen Seth? He was supposed to be working with Sayed and me, but no one has seen him today."

"Seth is bad cursed. He is not a volunteer childrens. I am only chaperone of childrens."

"I saw him," Chloe said, carefully tucking her lip gloss away in her pocket. "Earlier. He looked annoyed. You're Jan, aren't you? One of the kids was telling me about you. She said you're related to some famous artist, and that's how you got out of doing real work. Is it true you guys have your own well?"

"*Real* work?" I stood there dripping with sweat, my back aching from having been in all sorts of weird positions while I worked, the muscles in my arms trembling with fatigue from the four solid hours of painted-wall washing, my fingers raw from rubbing against the rough plaster, my fingernails torn where I had picked out little leftover bits of mulberry bark bandages that had been used to hold the walls together, and my head throbbing from having gone for six hours in one-hundred-plus-degree weather without food or water. "You don't think we're doing real work? What planet are you from?"

"Oh, come on, everyone knows you guys are just in there playing around while we do the hard stuff."

I just looked at her standing there, then shook my head and walked toward the mess tent. There was no use getting into a fight with the queen of the Lip Gloss People. Besides, it was too hot to argue, and I was too hungry, thirsty, and exhausted. In that order.

I collected a tray, a plate of some sort of lamb stew, and a big bottle of not-very-cold soda pop, and plopped myself down at a table next to the girl I'd met the night before.

"Hi, Sunita."

"Hi," she said as I popped the top on the soda and sucked down about half the bottle. She pushed back a thick black braid and gave me a nice smile. "Hot out, huh? I knew it was going to get hot during the days, but I didn't expect it to be this hot."

I averted the horror of a burp, and made kind of a half smile, half grimace sort of thing. "Me neither. Where are you working in the tomb?"

"In room Q. I'm sifting through the rubble looking for pottery shards."

I tore off a little piece of bread that sat on the edge of my plate of stew. "Pottery shards? That sounds . . . uh . . ."

"Boring?"

Her eyes sparkled as she grinned. I waved my bread at her. "Well, yes, but I wasn't going to say that. Besides, you get to work in the lower level. Sayed—he's the guy I'm working with—says it's much cooler down there."

"You're on the conservation team?"

I stuffed in a mouthful of stew (it was actually pretty good, but I was the first one to admit that after the day I'd had, a can of creamed corn would be just as heavenly as a triple-stuffed-crust pizza with everything but anchovies on it) and said carefully, so I wouldn't spew stew on her, "Yup."

"What sorts of things do you do?"

"Oh, tons of stuff," I said, swallowing my mouthful of stew. "Right now I'm cleaning the lintel over the doorway into room G. It's a picture of Nekhbet. You know her? She's the one with the vulture on her head. Well, not the whole vulture, just like a vulture-head thing. Kind of a vulture crown. Anyway, she's who I'm working on. I can even write her name in hieroglyphs. Want to see?"

"Sure."

I stuffed a bit more bread into my mouth, then reached for the paper that was tucked into my pants pocket. On one side it had instructions on how I was to brush the cleaning solvent over the walls. I flipped it over and started writing. "The wavy symbol, that's an N. And the footy thing, that's the K-H. The pot is a B, and half a circle is a T. Then there's a vulture at the end that Sayed says kind of reinforces the name as being Nekhbet's."

"What about the other letters in her name?" she asked, frowning at the drawings I made. I looked at them, too, and suddenly realized how stupid I'd been. I'd just proven to her that I couldn't draw worth spit. What if she said something to Kay?

I tucked the paper away quickly. "There are no vowels in hieroglyphs, just consonants."

"Oh. Have you tried to write your name in hiero-glyphs?"

"Nope. So, what do you with the pottery?"

"As little as possible. What was Dag going off on you about this morning?"

I rolled my eyes. "What *wasn't* she going off about? Anything and everything. Do you know that she spent the entire trip here yammering on and on and on about curses and our responsibilities, and how if we stepped out of line at all she could send us home without us being able to do anything? What's with that?"

She grinned. "She's one of those power Nazis."

"You got that right." I spent the next half hour talking to Sunita, eating, and drinking two bottles of pop. I still felt a bit guilty about caving and breaking my fast, but looking around the mess tent at the twenty or so other non-Muslim workers who were eating, I realized I wasn't the only one who couldn't take the heat without food and water. By the time lunch was over, I felt better about the whole thing.

Until I walked out of the tent and ran into Seth.

"Oh, uh . . . hi," I said, desperately trying to stuff a bottle of water into the back pocket of my jeans, but I wasn't wearing jeans, I was wearing the hideous white cotton pants that all of the conservationists wore, and which made me look like the Pillsbury Doughgirl. So instead I stuffed it behind me into the waistband. "Um. There you are. I missed you this morning. Um . . . well, I didn't actually *miss* you, because you weren't at work like Sayed said you were supposed to be, but I missed you as in . . . er . . . not miss, as in, like, I'm madly in love with you and missed you because I didn't see you and I couldn't stop thinking about you and wondered what you were doing and whether you were wearing another muscle tee—and you are; isn't that, like, weird?—not miss that way, but miss as in you weren't there and I was."

The two glossy black eyebrows that curved above his eyes pulled together.

"I'm babbling, aren't I?"

"Yes," he answered.

"I thought so. My mom says I talk first and think later, which is kind of stupid because you need your brain to talk."

People walked out of the mess tent in small groups, chatting with each other until they came up to Seth and me. Then the chatter dropped down to a whisper as people hurried by.

Everyone except Chloe.

"Hey, Jan, do you know you have a water bottle in your pants?"

"Yes," I said, a little bit defensively, true, but hey, there I was trying to have a meaningful conversation with Seth—in between my babbling—and she had to butt in and point out I had a bottle stuffed down my pants. Like I wouldn't know that? "I keep it there. It's handy. Is that a problem?"

"Whatever," she said, smiling a big old lip gloss smile at Seth. "Hi, Seth! Struck anyone dead today?"

He made a face. "Not yet, but it's only a little after noon."

"Good one!" She grinned as she strolled past.

I ground my teeth for a minute, then dragged my mind off the fantasy of tripping Chloe so she'd fall lip gloss first into the sand, trying instead to think of something to say to Seth that wouldn't make me sound like even more of an idiot than someone who stands around with a water bottle shoved down the back of her pants.

In the end, I decided honesty was going to have to do. "I guess you think I'm a loser, huh?" I asked as I pulled the bottle of water out from the waistband of the hideous white pants. "I don't blame you, because I said I was going to do Ramadan and all, but it was so hot in the tomb, and . . ."

Seth held up a hand to stop me. "Jan, you don't have to make an excuse to me about not fasting. You aren't Muslim, so no one expects you to participate in Ramadan."

"You're fasting, aren't you?" I asked, feeling worse than ever, as if I'd let him down somehow.

"Yes, but my dad is big on Muslim holy days. He

thinks they're an important part of our heritage." Seth shrugged and turned, starting to walk toward the tent where everyone left their backpacks. I walked with him, feeling a bit squidgy. I mean, there I was, my first day on the site and one of the dig hunka-hunkas was walking with me! If I were keeping a hottie score, this would definitely get me at least twenty-five points. "My mother says the same thing about Christian holidays."

I waved away a wasp that was buzzing around my head. "Bet that gets confusing sometimes, huh?"

He smiled and my stomach did a fluttery thing that had nothing to do with the stew I'd eaten. "I probably have the only family who celebrates both Ramadan and Christmas."

I stopped in front of the tent that had my backpack. "So your mom is how you learned to speak such good English? That's pretty cool. My mother doesn't speak any other language except Pick on Jan–ese. Hang on a sec; I have to put my water away in my backpack. Sayed says we're not supposed to take anything in the tomb but our tools and the solvent and stuff."

"Here," Seth said as I was about to enter the tent. He shoved the dirty black bracelet I'd bought at the bazaar two days before into my hand. "You left this behind last night."

"Oh, thanks, I'd forgotten all about it." I stuck both the bracelet and the bottle of water in my backpack, hurrying back out to Seth, wondering if he was planning on walking me all the way down into the ravine to the tomb. I racked my brain for something interesting to say so he wouldn't get bored and leave me. "Um . . . what did Chloe mean about you striking anyone dead?"

His brows pulled together again. I had the worst urge to stroke my fingers over the frown and smooth it out, but I quickly squelched that idea by reminding myself that journalists don't get involved with their subjects. "I told you last night—some of the people here think I'm the reincarnation of Set."

"Set? That's a god?"

"Yes. God of night. Lord of chaos. Murderer of his brother, Osiris." Seth walked quickly, as if he didn't notice it was at least a million degrees out in the sun. I shoved on the straw hat I'd pulled from my backpack, and trotted after him as he started down the long incline to the valley that held the tomb, praying that I wouldn't melt into a big puddle of sweat before we got to the bottom.

"Oh. Sounds like bad news. Why do they think you're his reincarnation?"

Seth shot me a scowly look, slowing down when he noticed me mopping at my face with the edge of my white T-shirt. "I'm sorry; I forgot that you're new here and probably haven't gotten used to the heat."

"That's okay; sweating is good for you. My sister Kara says you can lose all sorts of weight that way."

He came to a sudden stop even though we were only midway down the path. I slid to a stop behind him, the rocks and dirt skittering around me. The people behind had to edge around us when Seth stood with his arms crossed as he glared at me. "Is that why you want to fast? You're on a diet?"

Chloe, Sunita, and the French girl whose name I couldn't remember were laughing as they passed us, Chloe shooting me a curious glance as she skirted a big boulder.

I turned fifty shades of red as I looked away from him. "Geez, if you said it a little bit louder, I think they could hear you all the way in Cairo."

"Jan." His fingers were warm on my already hot chin as he turned my face so I was looking at him. "I'm sorry. I didn't mean to embarrass you. I just wanted to know if that's why you were so set on fasting for Ramadan."

"Yeah, well, what if I am? What's wrong with that?"

His brown eyes were even warmer than the sun burning down on us. They started a little fire in my belly, a fire that seemed to zoom through my body, making all of me go tingly. "You shouldn't use Ramadan as an excuse to diet, Jan. That's not what it's about."

I made an exasperated noise, not caring if the people trying to get around us heard me. "Oh, great, so now I'm violating some Ramadan rule?"

"It's just that Ramadan is a holy month, a time that is supposed to be dedicated to prayers."

"So I can fast and pray, but not diet, is that it? Criminy dutch, Seth, look at me! I look like the something out of Attack of the Killer Marshmallow People! And these stupid white clothes don't help—everyone knows white makes you look fatter."

"I always heard that was stripes," a voice said behind me. "Doesn't Mom say she won't wear stripes because they make her bottom look huge?"

I turned to find Seth standing behind me . . . only it wasn't Seth, of course. It was his brother, Mr. Octopus Hands.

"Hello, Cy," I said, trying to stop my blush from going off the blush meter and actually igniting my face.

He grinned. He was dressed almost the same as Seth, although he wore a blue muscle tee instead of black. His hair, however, was pulled back in a long ponytail, and I wondered if the two brothers checked with each other before they got dressed to make sure they looked as identical as possible. "Figured it out, did you? Didn't think it would take you long. Mom says you're on the conservation team. That's a shame—I bet you'd like the work on the burial chambers more. It's great stuff, isn't it, Seth?"

The two exchanged glances. Cy's eyes were more or less technically the same as Seth's, but where Seth's had a guarded, somewhat wary look to them, as if he'd learned to expect the worst, Cy's eyes had a look that I always thought of as secretly laughing. It was as if he found something funny, but didn't want anyone to know he was laughing at them. My fingers tightened into a fist as his eyes laughed at Seth, a slight mocking smile curling his lips.

"Do you want something, Cy?" Seth said, his jaw tight as if he were fighting to keep from saying things he wanted to say. I knew just how he felt.

"As a matter of fact, I do. I haven't had a chance to talk to Jan yet, and since I'm not stupid enough to keep a girl standing out in the sun just to chat her up, why don't we go down into the wadi?"

"Wadi?" I asked, ignoring the hand he waved toward the bottom of the steep path. I might be so hot that you could probably fry an egg on my skin, but I did not like Cy. He just rubbed me the wrong way. Besides, I wanted to finish talking to Seth . . . for professional purposes, of course. Interview, and all that.

"The valley is a wadi, a dried-up streambed. Come on, Jan; no one will miss you if you're a few minutes late. Why don't you stop by my tent and I can show you some pictures of the burial chambers?"

Seth turned away and started to walk down the path. My brain went totally psycho on me, and before I knew what I was doing I grabbed Seth's hand and slid my way down the gravel and dirt after him to a more solid part of the path. Seth looked down at our hands in surprise as I smiled over my shoulder at Cy. "Sorry, Seth is going to help me clean Nekhbet. Maybe some other time?"

I made it to the bottom of the path without falling, dying of embarrassment, or melting away completely, all of which I had figured could happen. At the bottom Cy walked by us without saying anything, but I could tell by the tense line of his shoulders that he was pissed at me.

"Welcome to the club." I sighed.

"What club?" Seth asked.

"The People Mad at Jan club." I disentangled my fingers from his and headed toward the tomb opening, not wanting to look at his face. Either it would be full of disgust because I had grabbed his hand in front of his brother, thereby making it look like *he* wanted to hold my hand, or else he would be looking at me with pity, feeling sorry for the girl who was so desperate to have people think she was liked that she grabbed the hand of whoever was nearest.

I took three steps before he touched my arm, moving around so he was facing me, the sun mercifully behind his head. The gold bits in his brown eyes were all lit up. "Why did you do that?"

I heaved an inner sigh and hurried into my apology,

hoping to cut him off before he said anything that would make me cry. "Why did I grab your hand? I don't know. I'm sorry. It was stupid. I won't do it again."

"No, not that. I like holding your hand. Why did you pick me over Cy?"

I gave him a look that should have let him know just how nuts he sounded, a little curl of warmth deep in my stomach making me wonder if I had been out in the sun too long. "Are you kidding? This is a test, isn't it? It's some sort of a test to see if I have heat stroke and am still sane, right?"

His frown was back. I almost smiled at it. I don't know why a frown made me feel comfortable, but Seth's did. I think it was because it was so Sethy. "No, it's not a test. I want to know why you didn't go with Cy."

I shrugged and tried not to look at his mouth. All of a sudden I wondered what it would be like to kiss him, which was not how a journalist thought about her subjects. "I don't like him very much."

"You said that last night."

"Yeah, well, I don't like him very much today, either."

He stared at me for a minute like he didn't believe me, his brown-eyed gaze boring into mine. "You're the only person who feels that way."

I shrugged again. "That's me. I always seem to do the wrong thing. I'm sorry I said what I did about your brother, but I didn't want to lie to you. If you don't want to work with me now, I'll understand. I'm sure your mom will get someone else to help with the lintel."

"My mother named us for Osiris and Set," he said, and it took me a minute to realize he was back to talking about why people thought he was Set reincarnated.

"They were brothers. Osiris was the king of Egypt. He had everything he wanted because he was the oldest. His people loved him. His family adored him. He never did anything wrong. One day Set killed him in a fit of jealousy. Osiris became the king of the underworld, but the people didn't stop loving him. They hated and feared Set, and blamed him for everything that went wrong."

"Wow. That's kind of horrible. But why do the people think that you're the reincarnation of Set? I mean, your mom named you guys purposely, right? So it was just one of those things you can't help. You can take it from me; I know *all* about parents sticking you with a weird name."

Seth turned and we started walking toward the tomb. I tripped a couple of times over small rocks, but he slowed down so I wasn't trotting after him, huffing and puffing and making myself even hotter than I already was.

"They think I'm Set because ever since I came to the dig, things have happened."

"Really?" I stumbled over a clod of dried mud (AMERICAN TEEN KILLED BY CURSED MUMMY DIRT!), but Seth grabbed me before I could fall. "Thanks. What kind of things?"

"Thefts, mostly. Various artifacts have gone missing from the dig. But there are also injuries." He slid a dark glance at me. "Whoever I work with seems to get injured."

"Injured? Injured how?"

We paused at the bottom of the short path that led up to the tomb, set about twelve feet up the valley wall. At the base of the path Kay was sitting in the shade chatting with a small, dark man in a blue suit. He looked really uncomfortable, but I knew from Sayed that he was one of the officials from the Egyptian Supreme Council of Antiquities—the government organization that watched over all the dig sites. Kay nodded to me, but didn't stop talking to the official as Seth and I grabbed our cleaning kits consisting of three different brushes, a small bottle of solvent, and a handful of clean rags for dusting off loose soil and debris. Kay frowned at Seth, but didn't say anything about him wearing unauthorized clothes into the tomb.

"Last week it was Sherif, one of the diggers. He broke his leg when he was riding my bike." Seth ducked as we entered the darkness of the tomb. Although electric lights had been set up in all the rooms, they were special low-impact lights that wouldn't fade the paintings of the walls. It was a few degrees cooler inside the tomb because we were out of the direct sun, but those ancient Egyptians knew what they were doing when they built the tombs into the limestone cliffs—the insulating power of all that rock around us kept the tomb a nice, constant temperature: hot. "Two weeks ago Omar, the dig doctor, was bitten by a scorpion and had a horrible reaction. He almost died from it. A month before that, Enrico, one of the interns I was working with, went off by himself and had heatstroke. They had to send him home after he got out of the hospital."

I stopped in the big, empty antechamber. "Now wait. So a guy fell off your bike—it wasn't you who held a gun to his head and made him ride it, right? And the doctor having a reaction isn't your fault either. People have reactions. I'm allergic to bees but you don't see me blaming my mom for it, do you? And that last guy, he was responsible for his accident, too. If he wasn't wandering around the desert, he wouldn't have had heatstroke. It doesn't make sense for you to feel responsible. They were just accidents."

"I don't feel responsible," he said, walking past me to the room we were working in. "But the rest of the dig isn't so reasonable. Last night I found a viper in my bedroll."

"A viper?" I asked his back.

He answered me without turning around. "A horned viper. They're poisonous. Someone put it there, someone who doesn't want me on the dig any longer."

I stood staring at the doorway to room G, my jaw hanging around my ankles.

LIP GLOSS PROVEN TO CAUSE BRAIN DAMAGE IN GIRLS WHOSE NAMES START WITH THE LETTER C!

Dear Mom,
So, here I am, in sandy, dirty, hot, hot, hot Egypt. If you got a letter from someone named Dagmar saying I am in trouble, ignore it. You know me, I never get into trouble. . . .

Oh, man, that was so lame. Mom was going to see through that in less time than it takes to roll your eyes.

Dear Mom,
I'm here in Egypt, having a wonderful time. I'm sharing my room with a girl who's a hundred times prettier, more popular, and less hefty than me, and I've made friends with everyone on the dig. . . .

Except Cy, whose lips went all thin and annoyed whenever he saw me, or Dagmar, who lectured me last night about not having the proper attitude when I mocked her curse theory, or even Seth, who had managed to work next to me on the lintel for three whole days without saying anything but "Uh-huh" and "Hmmm" to my lively and entertaining chat.

Dear Mom,
Today the hunkiest hottiepants I've ever laid eyes on was so annoyed with having to listen to me talk to him, he brought in a radio and played loud Middle Eastern music all day. Can I come home now?

I sighed and ripped up the sheets of notepaper my mom had insisted on including so I could write to her every week. What was the use in telling her how horrible my life had become? I couldn't go home, or I'd blow my chances at writing a salable story, and if I did that, I'd be back to what I was before I came to Egypt—a nothing in a family full of somethings.

Besides, there was Seth. He was perfect story material, what with everyone thinking he was the evil god Set come to life, and sticking snakes in his bed, and all the accidents and stuff.

"It's just too bad he refuses to talk about it," I said aloud as I stuck my notepad and pencil into my backpack. I'd been spending my lunchtimes—those days I managed to ignore my body's cry for food and water and actually maintain the fast, which so far was only one day—working up some good ideas for stories.

"It's too bad who refuses to talk?" Izumi asked as she wandered into our room. "Aren't you dressed yet?"

I chewed off a tendril of dried skin from my lower lip.

After almost a week in Egypt, I was beginning to see the attraction of having protection on my skin. Maybe Chloe, Queen of the Lip Gloss People, was onto something. She never seemed to have wind- and sunburned lips. "Seth, and I was thinking of not going to the party. I don't have anything to wear."

Izumi checked herself in front of the mirror she had propped up against a partially closed shutter. "You have your skirt. It's pretty. And you must come. Kay will be disappointed if you do not."

"It's her birthday, not mine," I pointed out, oddly reluctant to go to the dig-wide celebration of Kay's fiftieth birthday. There was going to be cake and dancing and party games, or at least so Izumi told me, but the one person I really wanted to talk to didn't want to talk to me. "No one will notice if I'm not there."

"Kay will."

"Yeah, but if you tell her I'm not feeling well . . ."

Izumi shook her head. "That would be lying. Unless you really aren't feeling well? You didn't eat as much as normal at dinner, and you missed lunch today." She turned fully to face me, her eyes narrowed as she brushed out her long, glossy black hair. "That is not like you. Are you feeling sick?"

"No, I'm okay. It's just . . ." I stopped, unable to admit to her the truth: that I had figured Seth didn't want anything to do with me because I had broken my Ramadan promise, but even after I made sure he knew I fasted today rather than eat lunch with everyone else, he disappeared after dinner. His motorcycle was gone, so I assumed he'd gone off on it as he'd done almost every night, rather than risk running into me on the roof again. "I just don't have anything nice to wear. You're all dressed up, and Kay made a big deal out of saying she was going to dress up nice and stuff, and all I have is my Godet skirt and top."

"You can wear something of mine," Izumi answered as she twisted her hair up into a fancy chignon. She looked gorgeous, very adult and elegant with her hair up and her long white-and-gold gauze dress that would have made me look like a round Christmas ornament, but which made her look like an Asian angel.

"What, a sock? 'Cause that's about all you have that would fit me, and probably even that wouldn't fit because I have fat ankles."

She laughed "Jan, you're not fat; you're just . . ." Her smile faded a bit as she looked at me standing in the middle of the room with my arms crossed over my chest. "Robust. Do you know what you remind me of?"

"The blob?"

"No, silly girl. A Rubens painting. Rubens was—"

I waved her explanation away. "I know all about him. Instead of Trivial Pursuit, my family plays Name the Artist. Peter Paul Rubens was a seventeenth-century Flemish painter who brought a new appreciation of Italian Renaissance art with his lush portraits of large, fleshy people, particularly women. Thanks, but I think I'd rather be a Picasso, all sharp planes and no flab."

She shook her head. "No one thinks you're flab."

"Flabby."

"No one thinks you're flabby. You are the only one who sees a problem with how you look."

I couldn't help it—I had to roll my eyes at that. "Oh, right, so the fact that most guys stare at my chest and nothing else, or that I look like a light-skinned sea lion whenever I wear a swimsuit, that's not a problem."

"Jan—"

I smiled and gave her a friendly squeeze to shut her up. "I appreciate the pep talk, Izumi, I really do, but it's not necessary. You're going to be late if you hang around here any longer."

"Sayed is waiting to take us to the dig," she said stubbornly. "I won't go until you are ready."

I tried to reason with her, but her mind was made up, so in the end I pulled on the Godet skirt and ballet top and my non-tie-dyed tights. When I complained about having short, curly hair that made me look like one of those Cabbage Patch dolls Denise had when she was a kid aeons ago, Izumi pulled out a couple of fancy jeweled combs and pulled my hair back off my face. There wasn't enough of it to put up, but I did have to admit that having it pulled back made me look like I had cheekbones.

Fifteen minutes later Izumi, Sayed, Gemal, and I pulled up at the dig site. We'd been squished into Sayed's tiny car, which even I had to admit was infinitely better than walking the four miles to the dig. For one thing, the temperatures at night were starting to drop dramatically, which meant it was getting cold out late at night.

"I never thought it could be cold in the desert," I said as I rubbed my arms through the big woolen shawl Izumi had lent me. The mess tent had been converted to party central, with all the tables moved out of the way, a boom box playing old seventies dance music, and strings of colored lights hanging from the ceiling. People were wandering around outside with cups of punch and plates of cake, or were inside the tent, dancing.

"Luxor often has temperatures that are fifty degrees higher in the day than the evening temperatures," Sayed said. "Would you be offended if I asked to dance with you?"

"Offended?" I blinked at him, I couldn't help it; I was that brain-dead. No one had ever asked me to dance! I was always the one at school dances that hung out with my equally nondancing girlfriends. "Why would I be offended?"

He made an eloquent gesture with his hands. "You are not a member of my family. . . ."

"Oh, gotcha." He was talking about the fact that guys in Egypt weren't supposed to touch women who weren't in their family. "You know, the dig team is kind of like a big family, so that means for the next few weeks, we are related."

"Yes," he answered with a smile, "that is true! Does not Kay always say the conservators are a family?"

"Exactamundo!"

I followed him in to the mess tent and we danced for a while to the awful disco music, but even though I was really happy that for once I wasn't standing with the group of girls who weren't dancing, I wasn't wild with happiness. Why? Because a certain dig hottie wasn't there.

Cy was there, all over the place, dancing with all the girls (except me), including his mom. A short, baldish guy with a goatee and gold wire-framed glasses turned out to be Reshef (Ray) Tousson, the head of the entire dig. He'd been in Cairo doing some official work for the antiquities council, but had arrived this morning to spend some time at the dig, and to celebrate Kay's birthday.

In fact, everyone was at the party—everyone but Seth.

"Have you seen Seth?" I asked Ammon, one of the young boys who sifted dirt for shards of pottery. He was stuffing an entire piece of cake into his mouth just like my little brother, Toby, used to do, but at my question his eyes bugged out in a way that Toby never could manage.

"*Áram,*" he whispered, bits of cake spewing out of his mouth as he backed away from me. "*Masha'allah.*"

Áram, I understood (it meant evil). But *masha'allah* . . . I thought that meant "whatever Allah wills," which was used as a term of admiration. At least that's what Izumi told me. But why would Ammon say *masha'allah* along with evil? It was a puzzle . . . and I knew just who to ask about it. The only problem was, no one seemed to know where he was.

"They ought to call him the Invisible Man instead of an ancient god," I muttered to myself as I left the tent, wrapping the shawl tightly around me against the cool night air. I hurried through the collection of tents, peering into as many as I could to see if Seth was hiding away anywhere, but didn't see anyone until I came to the small latrine tent that I tried to avoid as much as possible. Pit toilets are definitely not high on my list of things I want to experience again.

"Oh, hi, Michael. Hey, have you seen Seth tonight?"

"He's over beyond the Muslim camp."

I looked out into the dark, just like I'd be able to see past all the tents and trailers to the section where the

Muslim workers lived. "He is? Why? Everyone is here at the party."

Michael shrugged. "You'll have to ask him that."

"Thanks, I will. Night!"

I doubled back to the supply tent that I knew held flashlights, and snagged one so I wouldn't fall off the edge of the plateau in the dark. Slowly I picked my way around boulders and outcroppings of the cliff until I reached the far edge where a cluster of small black tents clung to the ground at the lip of the wadi valley. Chickens made soft, sleepy *bruck-bruck* noises as I carefully avoided stepping on them while tippy-toeing around the tents of the diggers, occasionally startling a mangy-looking dog or a sleek, well-fed cat. A small black-and-white goat bleated at me when I flashed the light on him. I was just about to yell out Seth's name when a tiny flash of light winked in the distance. The moon was out, almost full now, making it fairly easy with the light from the flashlight to find my way around the far curve of the plateau to where a dark figure stood with a tall silver-and-white object.

"Cool, you have a telescope!" Seth flinched as the beam of light from the flashlight hit him full on. Since the moonlight let me see enough of Seth so I wouldn't step on him, I turned it off. "Sorry, didn't mean to blind you. What are you looking at? The moon?"

"No. Constellations." His face was in shadow but his voice was deep and smooth, kind of like velvet brushing against my skin. I shivered, but it wasn't because of the cold.

"Oh. You know, I don't think I realized how much better you can see the stars when you get away from cities." I looked at the small, cold, bluish bits of light twinkling in the sky. "It really is neat. What exactly are you looking at?"

"Draco."

"The dragon? My brother Alec used to belong to an astronomy club, and I'd go along with him sometimes when I was a little kid."

Seth turned toward me, the moonlight softly caressing the black leather of his jacket. "Here Draco is seen as a crocodile. It represents the god Set."

"A crocodile, huh? I suppose that's like a dragon. What's that one?" I pointed at a bright blob of stars.

"The Triangulum. It is the symbol of Horus, supposedly set in the sky after Set murdered his twin."

"Ooookay," I drawled. "What about that one?"

Silvery light glinted on Seth's glossy ponytail. "Ursa Minor. It represents the jackal of Set."

"Criminy dutch, is everything in the sky about Set?"

His shoulders moved in a halfhearted shrug.

We stood there for a few minutes not saying anything, the distant sounds of KC and the Sunshine Band drifting out on the evening breeze. Seth didn't look at me; he just stood staring out into the distance, his hands fisted.

I pursed my lips, then realized he wouldn't see it. "So! I haven't had much of a chance to talk with you lately—"

"Jan, go back to the party." His voice was soft and flat, as if he were tired.

"What?"

He turned toward me, the planes of his face shadowed by the moonlight. "Leave!"

My stomach wadded up into a little ball while tears burned my eyes. "Fine! I will! You great big snotball!"

I turned and stormed off . . . about three steps; then realized I needed the flashlight to see where I was going. I marched back and grabbed it, figuring that as long as I was there, I might as well get a few things off my chest. "I have tried to be nice to you despite the fact that you've been as mean to me as possible. Well, I'm sorry you don't like me, and I'm sorry you have to work with me, but jeezumcrow, you don't have to be such a dirtwad! I thought you were supposed to be nice to females? I thought you were supposed to treat everyone with respect? I thought you . . . were . . . different. . . . Oh, poop!"

I mopped up the tears streaming down my cheeks and started back toward the main camp.

"Jan, stop."

I shrugged off the hand that had grabbed my arm, walking toward the distant lights and sounds of the main camp. "No, thank you. You've made it perfectly clear that you don't want me here. Despite what my mom says, it doesn't take a two-by-four to make me see the obvious."

"I don't want you here because I don't want you to get hurt!" he yelled.

I stopped. "What?"

He turned to me, his eyes grim. "I don't want you to be hurt. Don't you understand? Everyone I like gets hurt. It's what the diggers say—I'm cursed. I don't want you to get hurt, so I've avoided you."

He liked me? *Liked* me? *Really* liked me? A warm feeling of happiness grew in my belly as I stood there in the cool evening air watching Seth pace back and forth in front of me. He liked me! He actually said the words! I was *liked!* By the nummiest guy in the whole camp!

"At first I thought it was ridiculous. How could I be the reincarnation of a god? I don't feel godlike. But then the accidents started happening. Do you want to know how it started?" He didn't wait for me to nod before he continued, his voice as jerky as the sharp, quick movements of his hands. "My parents decided they only had enough money to send one of us to college in the States, and since Cy was the one meant to be the Egyptologist he would get to go. I was so angry I went to Cairo for a few days to cool down. I didn't tell anyone where I was; I just left. I had to leave or I knew I'd do something bad. When I got back Cy was just being brought home from the hospital. He'd had a severe case of food poisoning. My mother said he almost died. That's when the talk started—people said it was me, that I had somehow done it, that just like Set and Osiris, I wanted what my brother had, and I'd do anything to get it."

I sucked in my breath, nibbling on my lower lip, watching as Seth ran a hand through his hair. "It wasn't your fault, Seth. I get mad at my family all the time, but it doesn't mean I'm responsible when bad stuff happens."

He whirled around to face me. "This is different. You're part of your family—I'm not. When my father looks at me, he sees an American who doesn't respect our culture. All my mother sees is someone who makes my father unhappy. Cy doesn't. From the time we were small, Cy has always been the one people liked. I tried to make them like me, but he was always smarter, funnier, better. When I went to Cairo, part of me wished he was dead so I could have all the things he has. Even so, it wasn't until the accidents started happening that I knew what the workers were whispering behind my back was true. I *am* Set."

"Well, for someone who's a couple of thousand years old, you look pretty good," I couldn't help but joke.

He glared at me, a dark, velvety, brown-eyed glare. "I should have expected that attitude from you. Americans don't take anything seriously."

"You're half American, bud, so I would go easy on the bashing." I lifted my chin so he could see I was glaring right back at him.

"Are you insulting me?" he asked, stepping closer.

"If you think being American is an insult, then yes, I guess I am," I answered, moving forward until the toes of his boots were touching my tennis shoes. "I, on the other hand, believe that everyone except those guys who grabbed me in Cairo is the same, equal, not one bit better than anyone else."

He turned away from me as he spoke. "I'm cursed, Jan. I'm not the same as everyone else."

I gaped at him. With an open mouth and everything. "Cursed? First you're an ancient troublemaker god, and now you're cursed? What's next, the plague?"

I had to tug on his arm until he turned back to face me. "You're making fun of me again, but it's the truth. I'm Set. I'm cursed."

I whapped him on the chest. Not hard enough to hurt, but with just enough impact so he'd know I was serious when I said what I had to say. "You know what? You've got Set on the brain. You're Set-obsessed. You're a Set fanatic, a Set groupie, that's what you are. You really need to get a life, Seth."

His breath hissed out as the words exploded from him. "You don't think I want a life? I'm to be kept here, working for my mother while Cy is sent to the States to go to school at the University of Chicago. He is to be the Egyptologist. He is the golden child, the one everyone likes, while my wishes, my hopes are ignored because I am the evil one. Do not tell me to get a life, Jan. I am not allowed to have one."

"Oh," I said, my chest tight at the look of pain on his face. Even in the light of the moon I could see how much he was hurting. I've been called a drama queen before (by my brothers, who obviously don't know what they're talking about), but I knew deep down in the pit of my stomach that Seth was not indulging in a drama-queen scene. I just wanted to hug him and make all the hurt go away, but he was a guy, a hottalicious guy, and I was me, and although he said he liked me, I didn't want him back to thinking I was immodest or anything. "I'm sorry, Seth. That's not fair, is it? You should have just as much a chance at going to college back home as Cy has. Can you try for a scholarship, maybe? My school guidance counselor is always going on about scholarships. . . ."

He shook his head, his face stark. "I'm not a U.S. citizen."

"Pooh. Well, maybe something will work out. Maybe if your parents see how hard you're working on the walls, they'll realize that you really are serious about going to college. Maybe we could put in some overtime on the lintel? I bet if we got it done fast, that would show them that you deserve to go with Cy. We could work at night, after dinner. What do you think?"

He stared at me as if I had frogs sitting on my head.

"Didn't you hear me say I was cursed? That everyone I like ends up getting hurt?"

"Yeah, I heard you but"—I made a face my mother always called wry—"I just don't think it matters. Even if you are cursed—and I don't believe in curses—you're still you. You're nice, and really sweet even when you frown, and I like you. A lot. I'm not going to avoid you, if that's what you think. Uh . . . unless you really don't want me to be around, and you're just using that curse thing as an excuse, in which case—"

I swear to God, I didn't know what he was going to do until he was right there, his hands on my arms, his face blocking out the moon as I blinked in surprise. One minute I was standing there feeling kind of sick because I figured that he might just be using the curse to get rid of me, and the next minute his mouth was on mine, warm and soft and all sorts of other wonderful words that I suddenly couldn't think of because my brain stopped working. I just stood there and let him kiss me, too stupid to kiss him back, too stupid to even realize that he was kissing me until it was over.

My brain clicked back on then. Idiot brain. I touched one finger to my lips. They were tingling, and even though Seth wasn't kissing me anymore, my lips felt like he was. "You kissed me!"

He took a step back.

"You really kissed me. Wow!"

"I'm sorry," he said, his face going all tight and embarrassed. "I shouldn't have, but I thought you wouldn't mind. I won't do it agai—"

I threw myself against him, worrying for a second about what I was supposed to do with my arms (around his neck? his back? waist? left hanging at my sides?), but in the end, I focused on kissing him back. I kissed one corner of his mouth, then the other corner, waited for a second to see if he was going to back off or grab my boobs (like one of the guys at school did), but Seth didn't do either. He put his hands on my hips and pulled me tighter against him, his wonderful leathery-spicy smell wrapping around me as I very, very gently pressed my lips against his. It was the best kiss in the whole, entire, enormously big world. It went on and on and on, and in the end I slid my hands up his chest and locked them behind his neck, my fingers tangling in his long hair as I kissed him, and he kissed me, and we kissed each other out in the middle of Egypt, under an almost full moon.

"Wow," I said again when I peeled myself off his chest. I didn't want to stop kissing him, but I hadn't quite figured out how I was supposed to breathe with my face squished up against his, not to mention the fact that even with our faces apart, I was still having problems getting air into my lungs. My legs felt shaky, and my heart raced, and I wanted to sing and dance and stand at the edge of the plateau and shout down into the wadi that Seth kissed me! He liked me! "So I guess this means you aren't using the curse thing as an excuse?"

He laughed. It was a low, velvety, rumbling sort of sound that made me shiver. "I've never met anyone like you, Jan. You're funny and smart, and you're not afraid to say what you think. I like that."

"Even if I have bare arms?" I teased, still squished against him with my hands behind his neck.

"I like your bare arms," he growled, and turned his head to kiss the exposed part of my arm.

I shivered.

"Cold?" he asked.

"Not really. Well, okay, a little. But I like you kissing me, so if you don't want to stop, I don't mind being cold."

He laughed again and peeled off his leather coat to sling over me. I thought about telling him he should wear it, but it was nice and warm, and it smelled like him, so instead I just snuggled into it and watched as he put the telescope away in a nearby tent. We started walking toward the main camp, and I wondered if I should take his hand like I did before, or if that would be too pushy. Would he like it more if I made the first move, re: hands, or should I let him?

"What are you frowning about?"

The camp was just ahead of us. I didn't have much time before we would be back with everyone, and that meant I wouldn't be able to hold his hand. Not in front of everyone. "I was wondering if you'd like it more if I held your hand, or if you wanted me to wait for you to hold mine."

He stopped and grabbed my arm, turning me to face him. "Do you mean that?"

"Well, yeah!" I wrung my hands, something I didn't think you could really do until I found myself standing there on the fringes of the camp, wringing my hands. "I'm sorry if you think I'm really stupid or something, but this is kind of new to me. I mean, I know all about guys and stuff—I do have four older sisters—but you're the first guy who's really kissed me and all, and I wasn't sure whether it's cool for me to hold your hand, or if you're the kind of guy who wants to be the holder rather than the holdee. Especially since you're . . . you know . . . Muslim, and there are all those rules about touching people and stuff."

"It really matters to you what you think I want?"

I rolled my eyes. "Duh!"

He stood there silent for a few seconds, just watching me with those soft brown eyes of his. "You know what I like the most about you, Jan?"

I couldn't help myself; I glanced down at my chest. The ballet top didn't do much to hide the fact that I had what Scott, the guy at school who had copped a grope, called "bodacious mams."

"No, not that," Seth said, his face serious.

"Then what?" I asked, a little bit insulted. He didn't like my boobs? Every guy liked my boobs! What was wrong with him? He hadn't tried to touch them, not once, not even when we were kissing.

"I like the fact that you're not like most girls here— you do what you want, you say what you think, and you don't sacrifice your happiness for anyone. You're the bravest person I know, next to my mother."

"Oh," I said stupidly, blushing like mad because of the nice things he was saying. About me, Jan James, girl idiot! The warm spot in my stomach spread out to my arms and legs, making me want to shout and sing again. I looked down to where his hand was holding on to my arm and smiled. "So that means you liked it when I grabbed your hand before?"

"Does it matter if I liked it?"

"Yeah, it does, because I wouldn't want to hold hands with a guy who didn't like it, but you kissed me first, and you said you liked me, so I think I will go ahead and hold your hand."

"If you want to."

"I do. Because I like you, too. You're interesting, Seth, and you're not like the other guys here. You're different." Pain flashed in his eyes. I grabbed the hand that was on my arm and twined my fingers through his. "But it's a good different."

His fingers squeezed mine. "We'd better be getting back before my mother comes looking for us. She hates it when I go off alone."

"You're not alone now," I told him as we walked toward the lights of the camp.

Just as I was thinking that maybe it would be a good thing if I were to kiss him, a bulky shadow next to a tent suddenly divided, two people stepping forward into the small pool of light from a nearby camp.

"Good evening," Dag said in a harsh voice as she hurriedly buttoned the top couple buttons of her shirt. She slid a guilty gaze to the small, dark man who emerged beside her. "It is night out most pleasant, yes? Mr. Massan was assistancing me. I had smut in my eyeball."

Seth said something noncommittal as we walked by them.

"I'm willing to bet you the smut wasn't *just* in her eye," I whispered, glancing back at them. Dag was patting her hair and fussing with her shirt in a flustered manner while Mr. Massan straightened his tie. "Who knew Dag and Mr. Massan were gettin' it on?"

Seth waggled his fingers in mine. "They've been doing that for months. Everyone knows about it."

I glanced back again, but they had disappeared into the darkness. "This seems to be the night for kissing."

"I thought you'd never ask," Seth said, pulling me into the deep, black shadow of the pack tent.

BOYS SUCK—SCIENTIFIC PROOF
PROVIDED BY TEEN JOURNALIST

"There you are! I was looking for you." Izumi glided toward me, carefully balancing a cup of punch beneath a small plate of cake. "Hello, Seth. Your mother was asking where you were. She said she couldn't open her presents until you were here. Jan, I brought you some cake. Where have you been?"

I handed Seth back his jacket as he mumbled something to Izumi before going over to where his mother was yoo-hooing and waving her hand at him.

"Thanks, but I probably shouldn't. It's not on my diet."

"It's a party," Izumi said, shoving the cake and punch into my hands. "You can stop worrying about yourself for one night, can't you?"

"I suppose so."

She was about to go off and watch Kay open her pressies (the conservation team had chipped in and bought her a pretty reproduction antique Egyptian vase), but stopped to give me another one of her tipped-head once-overs. "You look different. How do you say . . . glowy."

"Glowing?" I grinned.

"Yes, that's it, glowing. You're glowing. As if you have a very good secret. Why are you glowing?"

"Maybe I do have a very good secret."

She grinned back at me and gave my arm a little squeeze before leaving. "I hope it's a very *bad* good secret!"

I stood around and glowed for a bit before settling beside Connor to watch Kay do the present thing. I'd met him only the day before, but he seemed nice. "Hi, Connor."

"Hi. I didn't see you at lunch today. Were you sick or something?"

"Nope," I said as everyone applauded the vase. Connor was a bit pitty-smelling, but I figured he probably hadn't had a chance to have a bath yet. Izumi said that water was rationed for the people at the camp, which made me appreciate being on the conservation team. I might have to work in the hottest part of the tomb, but at least I could take a bath each day. "I was fasting. Ramadan, you know."

"Oh. I didn't know you were going to do that."

I made a face. "Yeah, well, it took me a couple of days to get used to the heat and stuff, but I think I'm okay now. How are you doing?"

"All right. It's fun here, don't you think?"

I smiled at Seth, who was edging his way toward one of the doors in the tent. Poor guy—I knew just how he felt. Kay made a big deal over him when we showed up, but it was clear from the worker's faces when he walked over to stand by Cy that they weren't at all happy about seeing him. "Yeah, fun."

"The people are nice, too." Connor looked across the tent to where a cluster of girls were standing. "What do you think of Chloe?"

"Chloe?" It was on the tip of my tongue to make a snotty comment about her addiction to lip gloss, but I was so happy, I decided to be nice. Besides, she wasn't really bad, even if she did make the snarky comment about me having a water bottle in my pants. And she could smile at Seth all she wanted; he liked *me*. "She's nice. Do you like her?"

He made that guy shoulder move, the half-a-shrug thing that boys do when they don't want you to know they care about something. "She's all right."

"Uh-huh. Right." I grinned at him as he shot me a questioning look. "You know, the moon is almost full. It's very romantic."

"Romantic?"

He stared at me until I nudged him with my elbow. "Yeah, romantic. As in, kissing."

His eyes got big.

"Chloe just went outside a minute ago," I pointed out, feeling very helpful and benevolent and all that biz. "I bet if you were to be wandering around, you would run into her."

He thought about that for a second, then was gone with only a "Thanks, Jan!" tossed over his shoulder.

I sat back, pleased with myself. I stayed pleased for the next half hour or so, while everyone ate more cake, guzzled punch (orange and mango juice), and danced more to gacky seventies songs (excuse me, disco is dead for a reason!). I chatted with Sayed, Izumi, and the French girl (or tried to), but got a bit worried when I realized that Seth was gone.

I had just left the tent, wondering if he was waiting outside for me, when Cy walked up from the path that led down to the valley. He stopped in front of me, the gold necklace of hieroglyphs—the symbols for a throne sitting on top of an eye—glinting dully in the moonlight. I knew enough after having worked in the tomb all week to know that was the hieroglyphs for the name Osiris. "Looking for my brother?"

"Um. Maybe. Yeah. Do you know where he is?"

Cy smiled, gesturing behind him. "He's down there."

I peered past him. The path to the valley floor was curved just enough that I couldn't see if anyone was on it. "Oh. Thanks."

"You're welcome," he said politely, but that smile was back in his eyes and his voice. It made me want to slap him, but instead I fisted my hands and started down the path, careful to keep to the side nearest the cliff face so I wouldn't slip and go off the end.

Midway down the path it twisted. As I rounded the big boulder that marked the turn, I skidded to a stop, feeling as if someone had just kicked me in the chest. About ten feet in front of me, standing with a flashlight shining up in their faces, Seth was kissing another girl, a girl who was wearing his leather jacket just like I had done almost an hour before, a girl whose lips were no doubt sparkly and well lubricated.

Seth was kissing Chloe.

His hands were on her arms, and he was kissing her.

She was leaning into him, kissing him back.

A horrible sobbing noise choked in my throat. I spun around, tears blinding me as I scrambled back up the path.

He was kissing her! Everything he had said to me had been a lie. He was probably laughing at me the whole time, feeling sorry for poor, pathetic Jan, who actually thought he liked her.

I don't really remember how I made it back to the monastery. I have a vague memory of walking down the dirt road that led into town (and past the monastery). I think I heard dogs bark, goats bleat, and night birds calling to each other. I barely recall stumbling over rocks a couple of times, but that's about it. The rest of the walk home was a blur in my mind, a long, painful, "my life has ended, please let me die now" blur.

I even pretended to be asleep when Izumi came in. I didn't want to talk to her. I didn't want to see that look in her eyes, the one I saw so often at home, the one that reflected what a pathetic loser I was.

I had a major pity party, one that lasted through the long, sleepless hours of the night and into the bright morning. Not even Kay coming in to check on me (Izumi was worried I was seriously ill) dragged me out of my wallow in self-pity.

"I think it would be best if you stay here today rather than washing the walls," Kay said, doing that mom thing with the hand-on-the-forehead-fever-check before drifting out the door. "You look a bit peaked, and your mother would never forgive me if I let her beloved daughter get ill."

Beloved! Ha. What a laugh that was. No one loved me, no one at all. Mom had Rob and all her other children, Seth had that evil lip gloss hussy Chloe, and I had no one. Not one single, solitary person would care if I dropped down dead right at that moment.

My inner Jan rose up in revolt at that point, all but gacking at the pity party that had turned into a pity marathon. *Who needs Seth?* inner Jan asked. *We certainly got along just peachy cheesin' keen without him until now.*

"Yeah," I said aloud, pushing back the thin blanket and getting out of bed. I snatched up one of the three sets of white tops and pants that had been given me for work in the tomb. "Who needs him? The dawg. It's not like I can't have fun here unless I'm hanging off his lips! I'll show him. He might be cute"—I peeled off my nightshirt and stuffed my legs into the pants—"and he might make my legs go all melty when I'm around him"—I slipped into my bra and white tee—"and he might be the champion kisser of the world, but that doesn't mean I have to let him make me feel bad!"

I shook out my shoes quickly (in case of scorpions), then shoved them onto my feet, grabbing up my backpack as I ran out of the room and down the stairs just in time to jump into the last van heading out to the dig site.

Fifteen minutes later I dropped off my backpack, slammed the straw hat on my head, and marched down the incline to the valley floor, all the way thinking of just what I was going to say to Seth when I saw him. If he dared speak to me, that is.

"Jan!"

I gritted my teeth and refused to turn around to see the source of that wonderful voice.

"Jan!"

Kay, who stood talking to Dr. Ray at the base of the

tomb entrance, glanced back at me as I grabbed my bag of cleaning tools.

"Jan, what's the matter? Why are you ignoring me?" A hand clamped down on my upper arm, a nice hand, a tan hand, a strong hand with long, warm fingers that fit so well against my fingers. . . .

I looked over my shoulder and glared at Seth. "Don't touch me, you man slut, you!"

He jerked his hand back, his eyes wide with surprise. I stared for a minute at the white bandage that was taped onto his forehead, but refused to ask about it.

"What did you call me?"

I leaned forward so his mom and dad couldn't hear me. "If the lip gloss fits, shove it!"

His eyes widened even more as I whirled around and stomped my way up the short path to the tomb entrance. I growled out hellos to the kids waiting in the antechamber for the two archaeologists before descending into another chamber, pausing for a second to glare at Chloe. She was complaining to the French girl about not having a bath for a week and didn't see me.

"Jan!"

I turned on my heel and pretended I didn't even notice Seth behind me hissing my name.

He grabbed me outside of room G, pulling me into a smaller undecorated antechamber that now held only a lot of sand. "What is wrong with you? Why are you acting this way?"

"I would love to tell you, but I can't because I am officially not speaking to you."

He looked puzzled and angry at the same time. "But you are speaking to me."

"No, I'm not."

"Yes, you are; you're talking. Right now. *To me!*"

"I'm not talking to you; I'm just telling you that I'm not talking to you. There's a difference. Got it? Good. Go away." I brushed passed him into the room where the conservationists were preparing to start the day's work. I set down my bag and grabbed one of the wooden stools that were stacked against a wall, ignoring Seth who came to glare at me as I flipped on the stand of lights nearest the lintel. Each wall had lights mounted on a floor stand that could be adjusted to a specific spot, so we could see clearly everything about the wall we were cleaning.

"You aren't making any sense. What are you angry about?"

I eyed the section of the lintel we'd cleaned the day before. The paint on the side we'd cleaned stood out with lush, brilliant colors—golds, reds, greens, browns— against a background of snowy white painted plaster. There was relatively little deterioration of the lintel, so there was hardly any of the ugly grayish-brown plaster that had been used to patch areas of the painted wall that had fallen off.

Seth stood behind me, glaring a hole into the back of my head. "I give up. Obviously you'd rather not work with me. Since you want me to leave, I will."

I shrugged one shoulder and decided it was too childish to pretend I couldn't hear him. I would respond, but only politely, as if he were an acquaintance, not someone I'd locked lips with. "I don't really care at all if you stay or go, but if you leave your mother won't be happy with you, since we promised her we'd have the lintel done by the end of the week."

"Why should she be different from anyone else?" he grumbled, but tossed down his cloth bag of tools and flipped on a second light.

I slid a glance toward him out of the corner of my eye. He was dressed today in his usual black jeans, but wore a bloodred T-shirt that had a picture of James Dean and the words *Rebel with a Cause* on the front. Seth was the only one who ignored the rules about wearing whites into the area we were cleaning. Although some of the other guys had glared at him over that, no one but Kay had said anything.

"Now that you're talking to me, are you going to tell me why you're so angry at me?" Seth picked up his cleaning rag and the small bottle of solvent.

I used my fingernail to pick at a tiny remnant of the mulberry-bark bandage that had been used to hold the cracked part of the plaster together before it had been stabilized. "Angry with."

"What?"

"It's angry with or mad at. The other way around might be grammatically correct—I wouldn't know; I'm a grammar weenie—but when people talk, they say angry with or mad at."

His hands flexed as though he were trying to keep from strangling someone at the same time he sighed heavily. "Are you going to tell me why you're angry with me?"

"It's not important," I said with much nonchalance as I brushed away a speck of splattered mud and started cleaning the detail around Nekhbet's golden vulture headpiece. "Why do you have a bandage on your head? Did your curse get you again?"

His shoulders stiffened at my words. "It wasn't the curse this time—it was Chloe."

"Chloe!" The word burst out before I could stop it. "What, did she crack her head against yours when she was playing *Tongue: the Musical* with you?"

He set down his cloth and stared at me. "What are you talking about?"

I lifted my chin and cleaned one of the gold-and-red tail feathers of the vulture headdress. "You know what I'm talking about."

"No, I don't."

"Yes, you do."

"No, Jan, I really don't."

I threw down my cloth and glared at him. "Then you are not only a dawg, you're a heartless dawg! That's the worst kind!"

"You're calling me a dog again?" He looked outraged, his eyes blazing at me, the muscles on his arms under the lovely, smooth, latte-colored skin bunched and tight.

"Not a dog, a dawg!"

He threw his hands up in a dramatic gesture of defeat. "You are impossible!"

"And you're a poophead! A great, big, fat, hairy one!" I yelled. The last word of the sentence echoed for a few seconds. I glanced around the room. Everyone from Dr. Paolo down to quiet, shy Gemal was staring at us with openmouthed expressions of surprise. I gritted my teeth together and forced my lips into a smile before grabbing my cloth and resuming work on the wall.

I ignored Seth the rest of the morning. As if that weren't bad enough, he ignored me, too. Inner Jan reminded me that Gram had always said what was good for the goose was good for the gander. I told inner Jan to shut up, and spent the long hours of the morning feeling miserable. Seth worked right next to me, his arm sometimes brushing mine, but I couldn't talk to him. My heart broke into little itty-bitty pieces, turned to dust, and blew away in the wind like some half-baked folk song.

By lunchtime I was ready to murder someone. At first I figured it would be Seth (staked out in the desert while wearing itchy wool pants, big mittens, a thick parka, and a fur hat), but then I thought about things, and I decided that Chloe was the one who was to blame. She was just the type to try to lure Seth away from me with her lip gloss wiles.

The hussy.

"Are you coming to lunch today?" Izumi asked me, just as she asked me every day.

I rinsed out my brush and put it inside my cloth bag, sliding a quick glance at Seth as I did so. Seth was tucking away his brush, too, his eyes wary. "No. Ramadan. Fasting."

"But you didn't have breakfast this morning! You can't go all day with no food or water!"

I did a half shrug (it was too hot for a full one). I was horribly thirsty, but one of the things I reminded myself was that artists suffered for their work, and journalism was a form of art. A wordy form. "I'll be okay. Kind of."

"You must come to the mess tent regardless," Dr. Paolo said as he and the rest of the conservators filed out. Usually the Muslims went to wash and do their noon prayer to Allah while everyone else had lunch. "Everyone must attend. Dr. Tousson has an announcement to make."

I couldn't help but peek at Seth again. He stood with his wonderfully fabulous arms crossed, the black and gold of his tattoo (hieroglyphs that translated into the name Set) standing out on his biceps. My fingers positively tingled to run up and down the sleek muscles of his arm, but I reminded myself that I was mad, and you can't fondle someone when you're mad at them.

"You must attend, too, Seth," Dr. Paolo said a few minutes later as we staggered up the incline to the plateau, all of us hot, sweaty, and tired from the morning's work.

"I have something else to do," Seth answered, shooting me a dark look before walking off toward the Muslim side of the camp.

Dr. Paolo said something in Italian as he shook his head. I fought the urge to go after Seth and see what he was doing, about to give in when Izumi tugged me inside the mess tent. I plopped down on a bench next to her, smiled at Connor when he waved (poor, stupid fool—he probably didn't know that Chloe spent every free moment jumping innocent guys and locking her lip-glossed lips onto theirs), and tried my best to ignore both the wonderful smells of the lunch being lugged in and the hungry rumblings of my stomach. I hadn't admitted it to Izumi, but I had eaten while she was having a bath that morning, so I wasn't exactly starving.

The Muslims lined up at the far end of the tent, none of them sitting at the tables. Out of respect for them, the big metal pans of food had been kept covered, but the heavenly smells of cooked chicken crept out and teased me until I had to swallow a gallon or so of saliva.

Ray stood with Kay at the front of the tent, both of them talking with the antiquities official, who wore another hot-looking dark suit, and a tall, dark man in a turban who had a gun strapped to his belt. My eyes bugged out at the sight of the last guy.

"Hey, did you see?" I nudged Izumi and nodded toward the group in front.

"What?" Izumi asked, craning her head to see around the people in front of her. "Oh! He has a pistol! Why does he have a pistol? I was told this area was very secure and that we would not need armed guards."

"Dunno. It's probably got something to do with what Dr. Ray is going to tell us."

Izumi looked troubled. "I do not like pistols. They can be dangerous."

"Maybe he is here to protect us from a wild tribe of nomad warriors who are planning on riding into camp and carrying off all the women," I suggested, thinking what a wonderful story that would make. (I WAS A TEENAGE HAREM GIRL!)

Izumi giggled and glanced across the room. "They would have to be very handsome nomad warriors."

I followed where she was looking and saw Cy sitting at a table joking with a group of girls. The smile faded from my lips as I looked around the tent. Chloe wasn't anywhere to be seen.

Neither, of course, was Seth.

Anger roared to life within me again, anger at both of them. For a few minutes I didn't know who I most wanted to see strapped out in the desert covered with poisonous man-o'-war jellyfish, Chloe or Seth, but after a few minutes of imagining them both being eaten, I finally settled on Chloe. I had trusted Seth before she came into the picture. Given that I knew her type (man stealer), I would allow Seth to offer an explanation before I continued with my torture fantasy.

Ray interrupted my dark thoughts by clapping his hands and calling for order. "I apologize for delaying you from your lunch or prayers, but my announcement is an important one. We'll just wait for . . . Ah, there she is."

Dag entered the tent, looking a bit surprised at the sight of everyone gathered in the tent. Even though the mess tent was made up of open-meshed fabric to allow the breeze (what there was of it) through, with the whole camp gathered inside the heat and humidity levels rose until my white tee was plastered to my chest and back.

"What here is happening with pipples?" Dag asked as she stopped next to me, glancing around at everyone. When her eyes landed on the guy with the gun, she sucked in her breath in a long hiss. Izumi turned at the noise.

"Someone else who doesn't like guns," I whispered to her as I nodded toward Dag.

"It is with much regret that I must announce that a significant loss has been discovered. One of the artifacts recovered from the tomb has been stolen from the artifacts trailer."

"Not another one?" Michael said behind me to one of the diggers. "That makes three in as many months, doesn't it?"

I didn't hear the reply because Dr. Ray was holding up a glossy picture of an object. An object I immediately recognized. An object that was horribly familiar.

An object that was stolen—and currently resided in my backpack.

"Cheese on rye," I whispered, my stomach twisting

into a ball. What if the guy with the gun was there to arrest me for having stolen property? I could just *see* the headline—MUMMY'S CURSE SENDS INNOCENT TEEN TO JAIL! Eeeek! How could I be a journalist if I was in jail?

"As you can see, it is a onyx bracelet decorated with lapis and mother-of-pearl. It is known as the Handmaiden of Tekhnet. The small bird on top is of lapis, while the glyphs on the side offer a prayer to the god Set. If you have seen this bracelet anywhere, anywhere at all, I ask that you notify me. This gentleman is from the Supreme Council of Antiquities." He gestured toward the turbaned man with a gun. "He is here with Mr. Massan to investigate the theft, so I ask that you give them your fullest cooperation. Thank you."

The Handmaiden! Goose bumps rippled down my arms and back as I remembered the horrible dark alley in Cairo where the Scandinavian guys had demanded I give them the handmaiden. It was the *bracelet* they were after! The bracelet the old man had insisted I take . . . My breath hissed in a silent gasp as I realized something I'd been too stupid to see before—the old man had given me the bracelet by mistake. That's why Hans and Franz came after me—which meant there was a whole lot more going on than just artifact theft.

"Thank God I'm here to figure it out," I whispered to myself, visions of journalistic fame and glory filling my mind.

"It is curse most terribly!" Dag said loudly over the buzz of conversation that started the second Dr. Ray turned away. "It is curse of Tekhnet and Tekhen, mummies dead! I warn of keepings of cursed objects! They must to burn! You must to destroy before on all pipples becomes the curse evil!"

Dr. Ray smiled with weary resignation. "As I've explained before, our goal is to preserve the past in its entirety, not destroy those parts you find distasteful."

"Is much wrong!" Dag said, stalking toward him. "Is curse not claimed already enough victims?"

"There is no curse," he said gently. "That is just superstitious silliness—"

"Is not true! Curse is written on top entrance to tomb! All here have feared it. Pipples working into tomb are doomed!"

"It is traditional for tombs to have a curse written to discourage tomb robbers, but it has no real effect—" Ray started to explain, but Dag cut him off again.

"No real effect? Your son it is not who is being cursed?"

Cy's eyebrows rose as everyone turned to look at him.

"No," Dag yelled, her hands gesticulating wildly as she spoke. "Not him. Other son. *Evil* son! Evil son is taken by curse!"

Murmurs of "*Masha'allah!*" whispered softly from the far side of the tent.

"Now you know that is just nonsense, Dag. It's the heat—it's making everyone cranky today. Why don't you lie down in the hospital tent for a bit until you feel better?" Kay bustled over to Dag making soothing noises. She took the backpack that Dag had dropped and shoved it at one of the girls sitting at a nearby table. "Sue, dear, put this in the pack tent, would you? Come along, Dag. You'll feel so much better after you rest for a bit." We all watched as she gently steered Dag out of the tent. Dag continued to shout about the curse until the two women disappeared into a tent with a big red cross painted on the side.

"I'm sure I do not need to say again that there is no curse on either the tomb or the objects contained with in it," Dr. Ray said smoothly, a dull sheen of sweat glistening on the top of his bald head. "I do insist that if you have seen the bracelet, you tell me. I will be in the cleaning trailer during the rest of the day."

Conversation erupted as Dr. Ray said something else to the two men who waited with him before all three marched out of the tent. The Muslim workers followed, heading for their camp. The serving boy peeled off the lids to the food, and everyone else lined up to gather trays and plates, chattering madly about what had just happened.

I sat there feeling sick to my stomach as a horrible thought occurred to me. "What . . . uh . . . what do you think they'll do to the person who stole that bracelet?" I asked Izumi as she stood up and smoothed down her white pants. I stood up as well, worrying about the bracelet. What on earth was I going to do with it while I investigated the story? If anyone found I had it, I would be in deep doo-doo, which meant I had to get rid of it as quickly as possible.

I froze as a second horrible thought struck me: What about Seth? He knew I had the bracelet! What if he told on me?

"What will they do? I don't know. Something bad," Izumi said, giving me an odd look.

"You don't think they'd do anything really awful if it were someone like, you know, a tourist?"

She frowned. "If the person stole it, then the police would probably be called, but if someone had just seen it, then probably Dr. Ray and Mr. Massan would only talk to that person to find out what they knew."

"Oh." I nibbled on my lip for a few seconds, my stomach still doing somersaults, not even the sight of Connor sitting down with a plate of grilled chicken and vegetables making me hungry.

"Is there anything you want to tell me?" Izumi asked, putting her hand on my arm.

"No. I was just wondering," I answered, giving her a feeble smile.

She said nothing for a few seconds, then pressed my arm and mumbled something about my being able to tell her if I were in trouble.

"Trouble, that's the understatement of the year," I said to myself as I left the mess tent, heading straight for the small tent where the dig crew parked their backpacks. Everyone was at lunch or at prayers, so no one saw me as I squatted down before my pack, pulling out my notebook, bottles of water (which I had to avoid looking at in case I broke down and drank some), tissues, a crumbled candy bar, five pens, and an extra T-shirt (Kay was a fanatic about us wearing only clean clothes into the tomb, which was really stupid, because the place was made of dirt!), and finally, at the bottom I found the bracelet wrapped up in a scarf Izumi had lent me and I'd forgotten to give back. "So. You're real. And stolen."

I turned the bracelet over in my hands. It still looked like a dirty black bracelet with a blue blob on the top, but as I ran a finger down one side, I recognized the symbols that read Set: the curvy reedlike plant, a chick, a half circle, two slash marks, and the weird half-animal, half-man figure that Dr. Paolo said was called the Set animal. If I had any doubt before—and I didn't, not really—seeing Set's name carved into the onyx wiped it away. This was the bracelet that had been stolen from the antiquities trailer. But how had it ended up in a shop in Cairo? Why had the old guy given it to me instead of Blondie or Erik? While we were at it, who were they? And just what was Seth doing in the shop the night the bracelet was passed on to me? Was it coincidence that he was in the same shop as an artifact stolen from the dig, or did someone else know he would be there, and tried to make it look like he had something to do with the thefts? Or worse yet, was he responsible for stealing the bracelet himself?

No. I refused to believe that.

"I don't care what anyone says; I don't believe he's a thief," I said out loud, the sound of my voice making me feel a little less alone. "He might be a dawg, but he's no thief."

Despite the worry that burbled within me each time I thought about what the bracelet meant, hope rose at the thought that I might be able to uncover the truth. I tucked the bracelet away in my pants pocket and put my pack back as I stood up. Oh, I knew what I should do—I should march right up to Dr. Ray and hand the bracelet over, explaining how I ended up getting it. I hesitated to do that, though. It wasn't that I thought I'd be in too much trouble if I turned it in (surely the old guy in the shop would verify that he'd sold it to me); what I was worried about was how the whole thing would look for a certain long-haired, tattooed, two-timing hottie.

"Not that he deserves to be rescued after playing kissy-face with Chloe, but a good journalist doesn't mind martyring herself for a story," I told myself as I headed out of the tent. "I'll just ask him what he was doing at the shop, and whether he knew anything about the brace— Oh! That . . . that . . . oh!"

I jumped behind the tent nearest me, squatting down to peer around it as I watched Seth and Chloe approach. Chloe was laughing and reached up to touch the bandage on Seth's forehead. He jerked away, but I noticed he didn't leave her; he just kept walking while she chatted and giggled and flirted like mad with him.

All thoughts of turning the bracelet over to Ray disappeared in that moment. I waited until Seth and Chloe ducked into the pack tent before racing behind it to the tent flying a Swedish flag. Chloe had complained the night before about having to sleep in Dag's tent. *Then* I had felt pity for her, but now . . . I scanned the area quickly, but no one was around. Without waiting to think about whether or not it was fair of me to do what I was going to do, I slipped into the tent and eyed the three cots. The bedroll on one of them was tightly rolled (had to be Dag's), another was neat, but unremarkable (probably belonged to the third girl), and the last was a mess, with dirty, wrinkled clothes piled on top and a stack of glossy magazines scattered beneath it.

"Probably lip-gloss catalogs." I snorted, stuffing the bracelet beneath her pillow. "We'll just see how those sparkly lips of yours laugh their way out of this! Bwaha-hahahah!"

FLOWERS CAN KILL!

"Morning! Oooh, breakfast, num. So has there been any news of that cursed bracelet being found?" I asked just as I had asked every morning for the last three days. I grabbed a bagel, scooped some chopped fruit into a bowl, added a dollop of yogurt and a sprinkling of granola, and poured myself a cup of the hot, syrupy mint tea that everyone in Egypt seemed to drink.

"The bracelet?" Dr. Paolo looked up, frowned in concentration, then shook his head and returned to the process of stuffing his face. "No. It has not yet been found."

"Oh." I stirred the fruit and granola and yogurt together as I avoided Izumi's eyes. Although she hadn't said anything more to me about the bracelet or asked if I had something to tell her, I knew she knew I knew where it was.

I scarfed my breffie down in record time, and ran back to my room to grab my notebook, quickly flipping through it to read through the interviews I'd done over the last couple of days.

January James's Investigative Notes Regarding Theft of Handmaiden of Tekhnet (Ugly Black Bracelet)

Interview with Dr. Reshed Tousson (a.k.a. Dr. Ray): Dr. Ray said bracelet had been locked up in artifacts trailer along with other finds. Seems to be really angry that it's gone, so I don't think he's the guilty person. Asked him who had keys to trailer, and he said he did, Mr. Massad did (guy in black suit from the Egyptian Supreme Council of Antiquities), Dr. Battista (the head archaeologist) did, and Cy had one, as well.

Suspect list: Dr. Ray (He could have stolen it without anyone knowing.)
            Mr. Massad
            Dr. Battista
            Cy

Interview with Mr. Massad: Mr. Massad was really snotty, and told me he didn't have time to talk to me. I followed him when he went to the latrine tent, and stood outside it asking him questions until he finally caved and said that he had seen the bracelet only twice before it disappeared. He said it was worth a fortune, and that he had no idea who could have taken it. He also said that once the dig artifacts have been cleaned, cataloged, photographed, measured, and all that stuff, then he became responsible for them. Once the dig season is over, all the artifacts will be taken to the antiquities council people and later put in a museum.

Then he said rude things about school newspapers, which I ignored because I'm not really writing this article for my school's paper, as I said I was. Felt guilty about lying to him, but it was a lie for a good reason, so it doesn't count.

Suspect list: ~~Dr. Ray~~
~~Mr. Massad~~ (If he wanted to steal it, he could take it at the end of the dig season.)
Dr. Battista
Cy

Interview with Dr. Battista:
Spent half hour sitting on rock listening to Dr. Battista go on and on and on and on about the stupid bracelet. It's evidently really valuable, which makes me sorry I stuffed it under Chloe's pillow. What if she sells it and makes millions of dollars? January James, wonder idiot. Dr. Battista then talked about how exciting the finds in the burial chamber are, and how unique it is to find a tomb of a manicurist, and why it's going to make her career, yadda yadda yadda. Nice lady, but way too serious. Don't think she's guilty, although she could be.

Suspect list: ~~Dr. Ray~~
~~Mr. Massad~~

Dr. Battista (Might be guilty, might not. Must do more investigation.)
Cy

Interview with Cy:
Grilled him re: the bracelet after dinner, at the dig site. Tried to kiss me. Slapped him. He's obviously the thief.

Suspect list: ~~Dr. Ray~~
~~Mr. Massad~~
Dr. Battista
Cy (*Ding ding ding!* Guilty! Now just need to find proof.)

Of course! Cy was guilty! Cy was the thief! It made perfect sense! Wasn't Cy the one who received mysterious packages of money in Cairo? Hadn't he mentioned going to the shop? Who else took such pleasure in having his twin blamed for his actions? Clearly he was setting Seth up to take the fall, although so far no one but me seemed to know Seth had been at the shop in Cairo that night. As much as he was disliked and feared by everyone, I just knew that if people found out he had been there, he'd be hauled off with no questions asked. Except Kay. She would probably ask questions.

I chewed my pen for a few minutes trying to figure out how I was going to prove Cy was guilty, but had to stop when Kay yelled for me to get in the van. On the way in to the site I stopped worrying about proving Cy guilty, and started worrying about the bracelet. Why hadn't anyone mentioned Chloe's having it? It had been three whole days since I planted the horrible thing on her . . . she must have found it by now! Why hadn't there been a big fuss? Why didn't they at least drag her to Dr. Ray's tent and yell at her for a bit?

I gnawed on my lower lip the whole morning as I cleaned the last bit on the gold vulture headdress, wondering if I shouldn't go check to see whether the bracelet was still under Chloe's pillow. What if the thief—who had to be Cy—had seen me plant it on Chloe's bed, and had stolen it back?

"How are you doing alone, dear?" Kay asked as I'd made the decision to do a little covert work during lunch.

"Huh? Oh." I stepped back so she could see the bright, clean paint that I had just finished working on. "Fine, I guess. I've just got this little corner of the head-dress left; then I'll start on Nekhbet's face."

She gave me a mom smile. "You're doing wonderfully, but then, I knew you would. How can you help it with your artistic background?"

"Um . . . yeah." I stepped back in front of the paint-ing, not wanting her to start in on how talented my fam-ily was again. I heard it almost every night at dinner, and although each time I'd managed to escape having to show Kay my nonexistent leaf-mold sculpture, she left me feeling even more like a loser. I couldn't paint, couldn't draw, and now it seemed I couldn't even plant evidence properly. What sort of journalist would I make if I failed at covert activities?

She patted me on the shoulder. "I know it's hard work, but don't despair! Seth is back from his trip to Ar-mana, so I'm sure he'll join you this afternoon."

He was back from his mysterious trip that no one would talk about? He had been in Armana? Where exactly *was* Armana? "Oh. Uh . . . that's good he's back."

She gave me a sly look. "Yes, I thought you would like to know." She suddenly leaned close and whispered, "I don't believe I'm giving away any secrets if I say that when he returned this morning, he had a lovely bouquet of flowers for someone."

Flowers? Did she mean for me? Or was she talking about Chloe? I opened my mouth to ask her what she meant, but nothing came out but a squeak.

Journalists do not squeak!

Before I could get the squeaking stopped, Kay patted my cheek, then moved on to check with the rest of the team. Even though she did no actual conservation work herself, she made a point of coming in each morning and seeing what everyone was doing.

"Flowers," I whispered to Nekhbet as I cleaned off her vulture head. "But for who? Or should that be whom? Oh, great, Jan, your life is falling apart, and you're having a grammar crisis."

"What's wrong?" Sayed asked, pausing as he walked past where I stood arguing at a wall.

"Nothing. Sorry. Just talking to myself."

He gave me an odd look and moved over to his wall. I spent the rest of the morning waffling back and forth about what I wanted to say to Seth when I saw him. A lot depended on whether or not the flowers were for me.

I thought of begging a ride with the water truck as it went back to the monastery so I could see Seth and the flowers, but in the end I decided that my time would be better spent doing what I was there to do—writing a totally fabulous story about Cy, the antiquities thief. And that meant I had to find out what happened to the bracelet I slid under Chloe's pillow, and find proof that Cy was trying to frame Seth.

I waited until everyone headed off to lunch and prayers before emerging from where I'd hidden in the pack tent. Two dirty dogs wrestled in the shade of the mess tent, a couple of chickens were wandering around pecking lethargically at the ground, but no one else was visible. From the far side of the camp I could hear the chants of Muslim prayers. The mess tent was bustling as usual, with its wonderful smells and happy chatter of people not fasting.

I hurried off toward the tent with the Swedish flag, keeping my eyes peeled, but didn't see a soul. Chloe's cot was just as messy as it had been the first day—covered in dirty clothes, books, magazines, and a makeup bag that had opened and spilled out its contents on the blanket. I was just about to reach for the pillow when I heard voices. Chloe and Connor stood arguing just outside the tent. Connor left in a huff, but Chloe walked straight toward the tent. I looked around for another door, but there was only one. There was also nowhere to hide, so in the end I grabbed a handful of Chloe's clothes and sat down on the foot of her cot, trying like mad to think of a reason for being there. Maybe I could tell her I'd seen a snake crawl into her tent? A scorpion? A herd of scorpions?

Chloe came into the tent grumbling to herself until she saw me. "Jan? Hi . . . what's up?"

"Uh . . ." I blinked a couple of times, praying for the old oxygen thing to work, but it didn't.

"Ooookay. Did you want something?"

Yeah. I wanted her to keep her lips off of Seth, but until I knew who was getting the flowers, I couldn't get pushy with her. So I just looked down at the clothes I held in my hands and blinked a bit more at something I recognized. "This is Seth's jacket, isn't it!"

"Is it?" Chloe took it from me. "I guess it is. I should give it back to him."

Well, duh! I couldn't help but get a bit riled about the possessive way she fondled the leather, just like she had a right to touch it. "It is *his* jacket, not *yours*."

Her glossy, sparkly lips smooshed together in a pout. "Um, I know that, thanks."

Then again, maybe she *did* have a right to be possessive. Maybe the flowers were for her. Ugh! "Did he tell you you could keep it?" I asked, worried that maybe he had.

"What do you think? And what are you even doing here?"

"Me? Um. I was . . . uh . . . I thought I saw a snake. But I guess I didn't. So I'll go. 'Bye."

"Wait a minute! A snake? Is that the best excuse you can come up with for wanting to go through my things?"

I glanced at the wad of dirty clothes piled on the bed. "Ex*cuse* me? Like I want to touch your stuff?"

Her eyes were narrowed with suspicion. "What other reason would you have to be sitting on my bed, holding my clothes?"

"I told you, I thought I saw a snake," I lied, crossing my fingers behind my back. "Maybe if your stuff wasn't all over the place, people wouldn't have to touch it to sit down."

"We don't have padded wooden hangers and cold-storage facilities on the excavation team," she said in a snotty tone. "We're used to doing actual *work* here, not spending our time being pampered at the monastery."

Pampered! Oh! I could tell her a thing or two about just how hard it was working in the stifling part of the tomb, but I knew she wouldn't believe me. Obviously her lip gloss had leached into her brain.

And then she started caressing Seth's jacket.

"What're you doing?"

"Checking the pockets to see if I left anything in them."

I ground my teeth and was about to tell her what she could do with Seth's jacket (GLOSSY-LIPPED HUSSY RUSHED TO HOSPITAL FOR EMERGENCY BUTTECTOMY), when Connor popped into the tent. He started to say something to Chloe, then stopped when he saw me.

"Connor, you know Jan, don't you?"

Connor said hi, but I just gave him a sympathetic look. Poor guy, he obviously didn't know what a player Chloe was. "Yes, I know *him*. I just hope he knows the *real* you."

"Excuse me?" the two of them said together.

Chloe got a bit snarky with me then. I just wanted out of there, but before I could go she shoved the jacket in my hands. "Since you're so hot and bothered about the jacket, you take it."

"*I'm* not the one who's hot and bothered," I said with much dignity, pausing only long enough to warn Connor to be careful.

Once I escaped the tent, I ran back to my hiding spot (in the shade of the trailer used to house the expensive electronic dig equipment) and stood for a moment holding Seth's jacket, smelling the wonderful leather-spicy smell that made me think of the kiss we'd shared. It made me think of other things, too, like why he ran off three days ago without saying anything to me, and why he kissed Chloe and gave her his coat right after he had said he liked me. "And most of all, just what has he been doing in Armana?" I said out loud.

"Visiting my grandmother. Cy and I take turns visiting her when she demands to see us. This time it was my turn."

I jumped straight up, shrieked, and did a half twist as Seth's voice spoke behind me, his jacket flying out of my hands as I clutched at my chest. "Jeezumcrow, just scare me to death, why don't you?"

"Sorry," he said, looking fabulously kissalicious as he bent to pick up his jacket. "You were speaking out loud, so I thought you knew I was there."

"I didn't!"

A tiny little smile curled the very edges of his lips. Just the sight of it made my stomach do a couple of somersaults. "I know that now."

"Well, good." I tried to think of something brilliant to say to him now that he was back, but once again my brain let me down. I'm really going to have to look into getting a brain upgrade. At the very least I need to defrag it.

"You had my jacket," Seth said, looking down at it.

"Uh . . . yeah. Chloe gave it to me." My lips thinned as I tried very hard not to look like I cared that she'd had his coat for the last three days. The coat that he'd let me wear. The coat that smelled so much like him, just being around it made my knees go weak. "You went to see your grandmother?"

One glossy black eyebrow rose. "Yes. She's old and bossy, and my mother says that she's going to outlive us all, but my father makes us go see her every couple of months."

"Oh. Why . . ." I chewed on my lower lip for a second, wanting to ask the question, but not wanting to hear the wrong answer. "Why didn't you tell me where you had gone?"

His eyebrows flattened out to a straight line. "You weren't talking to me, if you remember."

"Oh. Yeah. That." I bit my lip again, miserable despite the fact that I was happy he was back, happy he was standing there looking so yumalicious, happy he was talking to me.

He tipped his head to the side, his ponytail swishing over his shoulder. "I asked someone about *Tongue: the Musical.*"

"What? Oh." I started to smile; then a horrible suspicion settled like a lead weight on my chest. "Who did you ask?"

"Chloe."

"Ha! That figures," I said to myself, but Seth heard me.

"What do you mean?"

"Nothing. What did the precious Miss Sparkly Lips tell you?"

His brows pulled together for a few seconds as he shook his head. "Just when I think I have a good grip on English you say things like that. Chloe said it meant a kiss, so I presume that means you saw Chloe kissing me a few nights ago."

I put my hands on my hips, giving him a good, long glare. Just how stupid did he think I was? And what happened to all the groveling I thought he was going to do? Crap. I bet the fact that he wasn't telling me he was sorry he kissed Chloe meant that the flowers weren't for me. They were probably for her. The witch. "Oh, right, *she* was kissing you! You were just, like, an innocent bystander whose lips just happened to be in the way as her mouth came charging through? You had *nothing* to do with the whole thing?"

His frown darkened. "No, I had something to do with it, but it wasn't what you think—"

"Oh, no, it never is, is it? Well, I have some news for you, buster." I straightened my shoulders and marched past him. "You don't know *what* I'm thinking!"

"That's the first thing you've said that makes sense," he said loudly as I walked away from him, heading for the mess tent. "Where are you going?"

"To get some lunch," I yelled back at him without stopping. "There's no reason for me to be fasting now, is there?"

Much to my surprise, Seth showed up to work with me on the afternoon shift. I had figured he'd go off on another one of his sulks or whatever it was he did when he disappeared, but he didn't. He was in the tomb working when I came in after lunch—a lunch I didn't eat after all. I sat inside the empty hospital tent and cried for a while, then reminded myself that not only do journalists not cry, they don't hide from guys who've broken their heart. Besides, I had my investigation to do. I couldn't cry and do that at the same time.

Seth didn't say anything to me when I picked up my brush and cloth. He looked a dark, hot look at me once or twice when his arm brushed against mine, or when we both reached for the squeeze bottle of solvent, but neither of us said anything for the remaining four hours of the day. If it weren't for the radio Seth had left in there, I think I would have screamed.

Although Seth and I weren't talking, I watched him a lot. I watched when he was called over by Sayed to look at a problem crack on another wall, I watched him from the corner of my eye while he worked, and I watched the back of his head from where I sat in the last seat in the van as we rode out to the monastery.

A ride that was the longest in the entire history of the world, by the way. I worried all the way there about what I would find. Oh, I had resigned myself to the obvious—Seth hadn't brought the flowers for me; he didn't really care about me; he was just a dawg, pure and simple—but a part of me, a stupid optimistic part of me, kept hoping that maybe he had brought them for me.

Izumi immediately headed off to our room once we got to the monastery. I was suddenly sick to my stomach as I slowly walked up the stairs after her. Seth stood in the courtyard below, his arms crossed, watching me for a second before turning and going to the far stairs.

"Why can't you just ask him?" I muttered to my inner Jan, who was yammering like mad about my being wrong in thinking he was being a jerk. "Why can't you just say, 'Seth, when you said you liked me, and you kissed me, and you let me hold your hand, did you really mean it, or were you just hoping I'd, like, put out or something'?"

I groaned as the words left my lips. How could I ask him that when I knew what the answer would be? There was only so much rejection a girl could take.

I headed down the balcony toward the room Izumi and I shared, my stomach churning with each step.

"Jan!" Izumi popped into the doorway, a huge smile on her face. "You'll never guess what is here! Flowers!"

I stopped, goose bumps rippling up and down my arms as hope swelled in my chest. The flowers were in my room! They were for me! Seth brought *me* flowers!

Izumi dashed back into the room, returning with a bouquet of pink and rust-colored daisies in a cracked white vase. "Look, aren't they wonderful? Oh, I wonder who left them? I haven't had flowers in such a long time! Daisies! I love daisies!"

My heart, which had been doing a happy dance in my chest, faltered, shrieked in pain, then wadded itself up into a ball and fell straight down to my stomach.

The flowers weren't for me. Seth had given the flowers to Izumi. Pretty, sweet, skinny Izumi. Izumi, who never argued with anyone. Izumi, whom everyone liked.

"Look, they were on my trunk. Aren't they pretty? I'm going to give them fresh water," she sang as she ran past me, skimming down the stairs, her precious flowers clutched in her hands. I staggered to my bed and collapsed on it, so crushed I couldn't even bawl.

"At least he didn't give them to Chloe," I said to no one in particular.

The next half hour has thankfully been erased from my

memory. My brain, taking protective measures to keep me from throwing the hissy fit to end all hissy fits, decided it was best if it just shut down and didn't let me actually think anything. I know that Izumi must have come back into the room, because later, when my brain started working again, I noticed the flowers on the small table next to her bed. And since she chatted happily at me while I got cleaned up for dinner, I assume that I must have been polite and said all the right stuff, because she didn't seem to notice at all that my heart was broken.

Again.

In the end, it was the eyeliner of the gods that changed my life.

An hour after we dragged ourselves into the monastery, we were all sitting around the big dinner table set up in the middle of the courtyard. Kay was telling Dr. Ray, who had joined us for dinner, how far we'd come in the conservation. "And Jan and Seth almost have the lintel cleaned."

"The lintel?" He frowned for a moment; then his brow cleared. "Ah, yes. Nekhbet. Excellent painting. I'm delighted to hear it's turning out well."

"It's really pretty," I said without looking at Seth, who sat across the table from me. I couldn't stand to look at him. I couldn't stand to think of what a stupid, idiotic fool I'd made of myself over him. "I like her eye makeup. I didn't know Egyptians wore so much eyeliner."

Dr. Ray smiled. He was shorter than Seth and Cy, and had a bigger nose and darker skin, but his eyes were the same as Seth's.

The rat.

"Oh, yes, the ancient Egyptians were very well versed in using cosmetics."

"Cleanliness and personal appearance were very highly regarded by them," Dr. Paolo added. "Much of what we know about their habits comes from discoveries made in tombs. Unguent vases have been found containing such items as a cleansing cream made of oil and lime, a wrinkle cream made of gum, frankincense, oil, and cypress, and the equivalent of hair spray made of resin and beeswax."

"Ew," I said. "Beeswax must have been awful to wash out."

"A lot of the Egyptians shaved their heads and wore wigs," Kay said, giving her pageboy a quick pat.

"They even had eye shadow," Dr. Ray said with a wink at Izumi, who was looking as gorgeous as ever. She seemed to know just how to put makeup on so it didn't look like she slapped it on with a trowel, unlike me.

"They did?" she asked in surprise. "What was it made of? What colors did they have?"

"Green minerals like jasper, serpentine, and malachite were primarily used," he answered. "They were ground very fine, then mixed with water and spread on the eyelids. It was thought to cool the eyes."

"And of course, both men and women wore kohl around their eyes," Dr. Paolo said.

"Kohl?" she asked.

"Really black eyeliner," I explained. "It's very cool. My sisters use it."

"Kohl was more than eyeliner," Dr. Ray said. "It was an eye paint made by combining malachite with galena—a grayish lead ore—and oil."

"I know that the men on the tomb walls have on eye-liner," I said, interested despite the fact that my heart was broken and my life was over, "but did the guys really wear it?"

"Oh, yes, most certainly. It was not only for magical and decorative purposes—it helped protect the eyes against the brightness of the sun, had antiseptic proper-ties, and discouraged flies. Both the eyeliner and eye paint were considered to be treatments or cures for eye diseases."

I grinned at Izumi. She grinned back at me as we both said, "We have to get some kohl!"

"Do you know that the ancient people even had a form of chemical hair removal?" Kay asked.

I looked at her to see if she was teasing. She looked perfectly serious. "They did?"

"Oh, yes. They were very clever. They used boiled, crushed bird bones, and mixed them with fly excrement, gum, cucumber, oil, and sycamore juice. The mixture was heated, then spread over the area where one wished to remove hair. Once it cooled, it was pulled off, taking with it the hair. Just like those fancy salon waxes!"

Ew! Crushed bird bones? Fly poop? I don't *think* so!

"Ladies, especially, painted red ocher on their lips, al-though many men used it as a rouge, too," Dr. Paolo added. "Henna was used to dye hair and fingernails."

"Wow," I said, staring at my bowl of chilled cucumber-and-mint soup, an idea starting to form in the murky depths of my mind. I glanced over to Izumi as she asked what the Egyptians used on their hair. She always had makeup on, even during the day, when we were working in the tomb. Her hair was always clean and shiny. She wore perfume every day, carrying around a little bottle of floral roll-on scent. I peeked out of the corner of my eye at Seth. He hadn't said much at dinner—although he had given me a couple of really odd looks—but he was watching Izumi as she told about an experience she had had with henna.

Are you going to stand up and fight for what you want? inner Jan asked as I dunked a bit of pita in my soup. *Are you going to just roll over and let him kick you in the gut, or are you going to prove to him that you aren't a loser?*

Why don't you shut up! I told inner Jan. *I am not so desperate that I want a guy who doesn't want me.*

Are you going to tell me you don't have the world's biggest crush on him? inner Jan taunted in a particularly snide tone of voice.

I snarled something rude to her and refused to answer the question.

You're a coward as well as a loser, inner Jan whispered.

Am not!

A great, big, fat coward who is too afraid of being rejected to even try.

"*I am not!*" I yelled, looking up in horror as everyone turned to look at me. I stared back at them, mortified.

"Jan?" Kay asked, leaning forward to see me. "You have something to add to the discussion?"

"No," I said, my cheeks heating up a hundred or so degrees as I slumped down in my chair, wishing the earth would open up and suck me in. "I'm sorry. I was just having an argument with . . ." *Oh, yes, Jan, brilliant. Just tell everyone you are arguing with yourself. They'll take you away to the nearest insane asylum and pump you full of happy drugs.*

141

"You were having an argument with someone?" Kay asked, a slight puzzled frown wrinkling her brow.

"Just . . . uh . . . me."

I dared a brief glance at Seth. His eyes were dark and unreadable, but for a moment I saw something in them that had my heart doing a couple of backflips. He smiled then, smiled right at me, and it wasn't a mocking smile. It was a nice smile. A very nice smile. I'd been watching, and he hadn't smiled at Izumi at all during dinner. Score one for Team Jan! I let my lips curl into a little tiny smile at him before looking back down at my soup, stirring it as I thought about those ancient Egyptians and their belief in makeup.

What worked for Izumi could work for me, couldn't it?

I snagged Michael after the second dinner was over. "Are you going into town tonight?"

He looked surprised at my question. Although Kay had said Izumi and I could go into Luxor if we had one of the guys from the dig with us, neither of us had the time to do it. Evenings after dinner were spent taking baths, washing our hair, washing clothes, and listening to the lectures Dr. Paolo gave on ancient Egypt. "Yes, I am. Do you want to ride along?"

"Yeah, if you can take me to a drugstore or department store."

"Drugstore?" He looked horrified, as though I had asked him to do something illegal.

"Yeah, you know, the kind of place that has makeup and stuff."

His shoulders slumped in relief. "Cosmetics!"

"Yup. Is there somewhere I can get some in Luxor?"

He chuckled and waved me toward the front door.

"You were listening to Dr. Ray's talk, eh? Good for you. No drugstores, but cosmetics in the market, yes. Come."

"Just a sec, let me get my money." I raced back to my room and dug out my neck pouch that held my passport and spending money, tucking it beneath my shirt before running down the stairs again.

"Jan. I want to talk to you," Seth said as he came out of the sitting room.

"Sorry, can't talk now. Later, okay?"

He frowned. (What else?) "No, it's not okay. Don't you have anything to say to me?"

Like what? 'Thank you for destroying me'? 'Hope you and Izumi live happily ever after'? 'May the fleas of a thousand camels infest your crotch'? "Not now. Tomorrow. Gotta run. Later, tater!"

I ran off before he could say anything else. If he wanted to talk to me now, just wait until he got a load of the new Jan!

MUMMY'S ANCIENT COSMETIC
SECRETS UNCOVERED!

"Jan? Are you coming? The first van has already left, and we're waiting— Oh. Goodness. Don't you look . . . pretty."

I grabbed my backpack as I dashed past Kay. "I'm ready."

"Er . . . very well." Kay shook her head as she followed me to the van, which held Dr. Paolo, Michael, and Gemal. I climbed into the back with Gemal, pleased with the response I was getting so far. Even Dr. Paolo was staring at me as if he hadn't seen me before.

Those ancient Egyptians really knew what they were doing.

"I've forgotten just what it's like to be sixteen," Kay murmured as Dr. Paolo continued to stare at me. I waited until he faced front before digging out my mirror and taking a quick check to make sure the kohl I'd applied hadn't smeared. Two gray eyes ringed with black peered out of the mirror at me. I picked apart one of the clumps of eyelashes that had formed from the cheap mascara I'd bought at the market in addition to kohl and green eye paint, and admired my eyes for another few seconds before tucking the mirror away.

It hadn't been easy hiding from Seth the night before, but I hadn't wanted him to see me before I could dazzle him with my . . . well, I suppose *great beauty* would be stretching it, but *clever use of kohl* wouldn't be. After the first application of kohl, my eyes were dramatic, dark, and mysterious—everything I hoped would make Seth think twice about Izumi.

I dropped off my pack and almost ran into Chloe as I left the tent. She was in the middle of putting on yet another coat of sparkly lip gloss, which was probably the reason her mouth hung open as she stared at me.

"Are you going to a party?" she asked, finally managing to close her mouth.

I frowned, but had to stop because my eyelashes were sticking to the skin above my eyes (I think the heat did something to the mascara, because it seemed awfully sticky and tended to make my eyelashes form spiky clumps). "No, I'm not."

"Oh. I wondered if you were going to a costume party as a raccoon."

"A raccoon?"

"Yeah." She drew imaginary circles around her eyes. "Raccoon."

"Haven't you ever seen kohl?" I asked, shooting a disdainful glance at her sparkly, wet-looking lips. "It's very cool. Guys like it much more than slobber lips."

"Slobber lips!" She gasped, and I could tell she was going to say something really mean, but I didn't wait to hear it. I pushed past and walked toward the path leading into

145

the wadi, mentally going over what I was going to say when I saw Seth. Although I had decided the night before that I was not going to stand by and let Izumi nab him when by rights he should be mine (I kissed him first! At least, I think I was the first . . .), I wasn't going to chase after him, either. I'd seen girls do that—Chloe flirting like mad with Seth was a perfect example—and I wouldn't lower myself to that level. Izumi seemed to have a technique that worked, so my plan was to be the Jan version of her. Janzumi, temptress of the Middle East; that was me!

I trotted past the mess tent, saying hi to all the kids straggling out of it. Honestly, they didn't have to get up before sunrise to eat, and yet the French girl, Sue, and Kathy (the girl who always looked like she smelled dog poop) were staggering out of the tent as if they'd just woken up. I knew this was their day off of work, but sheesh! "Hi, guys. How's the digging going?"

"Dirty," Sue snarled, shooting a glare at Kathy as she scratched her hair. I couldn't help but feel sorry for the dig kids. They didn't seem to be able to wash much, and their clothes were always dirty and dusty. At least we got to take a bath each day.

Kathy ignored her. "Hi, Jan. What are you all made up for?"

I tried to flutter my eyelashes, but stopped when my upper and lower eyelashes glued together for a minute. I pried them apart before answering her. "Nothing. We had a talk last night about ancient Egyptian cosmetics, so I thought I'd try them out. See ya 'round!"

I snatched up the linen bag with my cleaning supplies from the box, smiled brightly at Dr. Ray as he stood chatting with Kay and Dr. Paolo, then hurried up to the tomb's opening. Seth and Izumi had ridden out on the first van, which meant they had quality time together.

"Morning!" I called out once I entered room G.

Izumi, who had her head tipped toward Seth as she listened to him, turned around and started to say something, but choked to a stop and stared at me instead. I smiled to myself, pleased that a little makeup could have such an effect. Seth stared at me too, and I just about did a backflip when he left Izumi and came over to where I was setting up the lights and stool so I could work on Nekhbet's face.

"Why have you been avoiding me?" he asked in a low voice so no one else could hear.

I glanced over at Izumi. She was still staring at me with a kind of shocked look on her face. A little zinger of guilt stabbed me, making me almost feel sorry I'd decided to fight for Seth. But all was fair in love and war, right? "To the best girl goes the hottie."

"What?"

Seth looked confused. I gave him a shark grin and hoisted my butt onto the stool so I could brush off the day's accumulation of dust on the wall. "Nothing. And I haven't been avoiding you; I just haven't . . . um . . . seen you."

"You ran off last night," he accused.

I opened my eyes really wide to show my innocence. "Who, me? Ran off? Huh-uh, I just went into Luxor with Michael. We went shopping in the market."

His frown got even frownier. "I would have taken you if I'd known you wanted to go to the market. You didn't have to go with Michael."

"Really?" I asked, thinking I could probably win the

award for Miss Perfect Impression of Innocence. "I thought you were busy last night." *Busy breaking my heart by giving another girl flowers.*

His frown changed to an uncomfortable look. He glanced at Izumi (who had finally stopped staring at me and started doing her own work), then back to me. A fly buzzed around my face. I waved my hand at it as Seth said, "Jan, I want to explain about the flowers."

The fly buzzed past my face again. I turned away from him, lifted my chin, and started brushing the dust off the wall, pausing to snap the cloth at the annoying fly. "You don't have to explain anything to me. You can give flowers to whomever you want. It doesn't mean squat to me."

"Yes, I do have to explain." He took a deep breath and said quickly, "I never meant to give the flowers to Izumi. I brought them for you, but I didn't know which bed was yours, and they ended up on hers by mistake, and now she thinks I brought them for her, and I didn't want to tell her the truth because it would hurt her feelings."

"And, of course, we wouldn't want to hurt her feelings," I said in a tone that sounded really, really snotty, even though part of me wanted to dance and sing. He hadn't brought Izumi flowers after all! He'd brought them for me! I tried to catch the buzzing fly but it zoomed around my head in fast circles.

"No, we wouldn't," he said softly, "but I don't want *your* feelings hurt, either."

I felt awful. Izumi was my friend. She hadn't done anything to hurt me, and there I was thinking mean thoughts about her just because I thought Seth had preferred her to me. "I'm glad you didn't tell Izumi the truth. She's very sweet. But I'm also glad you didn't mean to give her the flowers."

He put a finger under my chin and turned my head so I was looking at him. "Truce?"

"Yeah," I said with a smile, feeling all warm and happy inside as he smiled back. For a second. Then his smile turned to a look of stunned horror as I glared at the corner of my eye.

"Jan?"

"Hmmm?" I asked, still glaring.

"Do you know that you have a fly caught in your eyelashes?"

I transferred my glare from the fly to him. "Well, of course I know I have a fly caught in my eyelashes! How can you have a fly stuck to your eye and not know it?"

His lips twitched.

"Don't you even think about laughing," I snapped. I held out my hand. "Tweezers."

He grabbed the pair of tweezers that we used to pull off leftover fibers from the mulberry bandages, and slapped them into my palm. "Would you like me to do it?"

The fly tickled as it buzzed like mad, caught in the tangle of eyelashes at the far edge of my right eye, the sticky snare of my mascara evidently strong enough to trap insects. "No, thank you. I always remove my own eye flies."

He said nothing as I plucked the fly free. It was almost as annoyed as I was embarrassed, but not even having a fly stuck to my eye could ruin my day—Seth had meant to give the flowers to *me!*

"Cy's band is going to play tonight after dinner."

"Your brother has a band?" He probably *stole* the instruments.

"Yes. Cy and a couple of the diggers. They're not very good, but it's better than nothing."

I brushed at the wall. "Don't you play with them?"

He shook his head. "I can't play a musical instrument."

I dropped the cloth as I spun around to face him. "Neither can I! All my brothers and sisters can, but I can't even play the guitar! I break strings when I try. Wow! That's, like, so freaky that you can't play, either!"

"I thought maybe . . . would you like to have dinner here with me and watch them afterward?"

My mouth fell open, but only for a few seconds. I swallowed hard. "You mean . . . like a *date?*"

His eyes were wary. "Do you want it to be?"

Uh-oh! I had to be really careful here. "Um, I do if *you* do."

He thought about that for a few seconds. "I do."

A breath I didn't know I was holding whooshed out of me. "I do, too."

"Good."

"Yeah." I smiled at him. He smiled at me. We smiled at each other until I figured we'd better do some work or else I'd throw myself at his head and kiss him until we both passed out from lack of oxygen.

The day zoomed by at warp speed, thank God. While we cleaned the wall, Seth told me about his trip to Armana and his grandmother. After lunch (we spent it sitting in the shade talking with Gemal and his little brother, who was a digger) I told Seth about what it was like to be the only talentless person in my family. I wasn't sure I should let him in on my secret, but he understood everything I said.

"The black sheep," he said carefully just before we were to stop work.

"Black sheep?"

"It is not right? Black lamb?" he asked, his eyes puzzled.

"Oh! You mean I'm the black sheep of my family? Oh, man, with fries on the side!"

His eyebrows shot up.

"That means you're right," I explained. "I'm so black sheep, I'm baaing."

"I am as well," he said, a little frown settling on his forehead.

"Hey, I meant to ask you—just how did you hurt your head last week?"

He swished his brush around in the little tin cup of water we used to wet cleaning cloths, shaking the brush before putting it away in his bag. "I fell off a rope ladder into the burial chamber."

"Oh." I eyed his forehead carefully. There was a small scab on it, but nothing that looked serious. "Chloe was there?"

"Yes." He looked up as I hauled the stool back to where they were stacked. "Why did you want to know?"

"No reason. I was thinking that maybe there was a story about someone trying to off you because they think you're an evil god come back to life, but that sounds like it was an accident, not a curse."

The minute the words left my lips, I could have kicked myself. Seth had been happy during the day, talking about himself and his life, and how isolated he felt from both his parents and his brother—something I totally understood, feeling pretty much the same—but as soon as

I mentioned the curse, he went all moody again. "Chloe is lucky I was hurt instead of her."

"You're not going to start that 'I'm dangerous to anyone around me' biz again, are you? 'Cause if you are, I'm going to ask Michael to be my date for dinner."

He looked outraged at that. "You do not take the curse seriously!"

I slung the cloth bag over my shoulder and gave Seth a look that should have said it all, but I knew he wouldn't get it (guys are clueless that way). "Curse, schmurse. You're not cursed, Seth; you're just a bad-boy biker. In case you don't know, that's good. Girls like bad boys."

He grabbed my arm as I was about to walk by him, his hand sliding up my arm underneath the sleeve of the horrible white T-shirt. "Do you?"

My stomach started doing jumping jacks as his hand, warm and gentle, stroked down my arm. "Like bad boys? Yeah. I like them *really* bad."

"So bad they're cursed?" he asked, tugging me close so that I leaned up against him. There was no one else in the room, but I could hear people talking in the antechamber. I didn't care, though. I just wanted to stand there smooshed up against Seth, breathing in the wonderful spicy smell that always seemed to surround him. I slid my arms around his waist as he wrapped his around me, making me feel safe and happy and a lot like I was going to burst into flames. Spontaneous combustion, that was it. I was sure I was going to spontaneously combust if he kissed me again.

His eyes went all dreamy as his head tipped toward me, his lips brushing mine.

"What's a little fire?" I breathed into his mouth as he

started kissing me for real. His lips were warm and soft, and made my knees go melty until I had to cling to him to keep from falling. Just when I thought it couldn't get any hotter, his tongue touched my lips. My blood seemed to boil as I let him into my mouth, prepared to back off if it got gross (I mean, it was his *tongue!*), but it didn't. In fact, it got better. His tongue touched mine, teasing it, sliding around it with little touches until I figured, *What the heck, I might as well do this properly.* So I did a little tongue dance around his and just kind of lost my head after that.

"Jan? Seth? Are you coming back to the monastery tonight, or are you staying for Cy's—oh!"

I sucked my tongue back into my mouth and jumped back from Seth. "Hi, Kay. Um. We were just . . . uh . . ." I glared at Seth, hoping he'd say something that would explain what happened.

"We were kissing," he said, not seeming to mind at all that his mom knew.

I, on the other hand, wanted to die right there on the spot. After I killed him, of course.

"No, we weren't kissing. Hahahaha! What a comedian. We were . . . uh . . . I had this fly stuck to my eye, and Seth said he'd get it off, but it was really small, and—"

Seth wrapped one arm around my waist and hauled me in close to him, his jaw set as he looked at his mother. "We were kissing."

"Yes, I rather thought that's what you were doing," she said, her voice neutral, like she didn't care. "Are you both staying behind?"

"We weren't kissing," I said quickly.

"Yes, we were," Seth said. "And yes, we're staying behind. I'll bring Jan back to the monastery on my bike."

"It wasn't really a kiss—"

"Very well. Enjoy yourselves," she said, pausing to give Seth a mom look I recognized. "But not *too* much, dear."

"—it was more a little peck— Oh!" Kay left the room without another word. I did the blink thing because I was feeling a bit light-headed after kissing Seth. "She left. Doesn't she care that I was kissing you?"

"No. Why should she?" Seth let go of me to grab both our bags.

"Well . . . I don't know," I had to admit, then decided not to worry about it. Life was too good to worry about something that no one else was worried about. I had Seth, we were going on a date tonight (even if it was just a date at the camp), and he was going to give me a ride home on his motorcycle. There was only one thing that blotted my happiness—finding proof of Cy's guilt. Would Seth hate me for proving that his brother was a thief? I decided that even a journalist deserved a night off, so I pushed that worry aside for the night and did my best to forget all about the bracelet.

"I'm so happy," I told Seth later, as we walked out of the mess tent where Cy and his band had been playing. "This was the best date ever!"

"It was fun, even if the music was awful," Seth said with a grin. "Cy's new guitar didn't make him sound any better."

It was a wonderful, clear night just like all the other nights, with a bright moon, twinkling stars, and a gentle breeze. Everyone was laughing and chatting happily as they streamed out of the tent, a kind of party atmosphere making everyone a bit silly. A couple of the girls were dancing their way toward their tents, singing together in voices almost as bad as Cy's and his band's.

I couldn't help but shoot Chloe a look when we walked by her. Seth paused to put his leather jacket around me when I shivered. Chloe just rolled her eyes and said something to Connor that had him laughing.

"Let me get my backpack and I'll be ready to go back," I told Seth as I let go of his hand in order to duck into the small tent that held the packs.

"I'll go start my bike."

"Okay. Be right there." I watched him head over to the area where the dig trucks and vans were kept, then opened my pack, looking for my mirror. So far the makeup had worked wonders, and even if I knew now that Seth had really brought the flowers for me, I figured it couldn't hurt to make sure I looked good all the time. As I reached into the backpack for the little round mirror, my hand closed on a similarly shaped object. It was round, all right, but it wasn't a mirror.

I pulled the object out and stared at it, my eyes narrowing with suspicion, anger, and determination.

It was the bracelet, the Handmaiden of Tekhnet. Someone—and I knew just who it was—had ditched it in my bag.

"Right, this time it's personal," I said softly, folding the bracelet into the spare T-shirt I kept in the pack, tucking it away on the bottom of the bag. "This means war, Chloe. Prepare to be defeated!"

EGYPTIAN CURSE RUINS TEEN'S LIFE!

"You're going to eat lunch today?" Izumi yelled as I set my tray down next to hers. All I had on the tray was a bowl of fruit, a spoon, and a napkin, but I wasn't planning on eating anything. I couldn't tell Izumi that I was there on an undercover mission, though, because then she'd want to know what my mission was (plant the bracelet on Chloe . . . *again*), and why I didn't turn it over to Ray (revenge, pure and simple), not to mention the whole story of how I ended up with the bracelet. I hadn't even told Seth about it yet. He didn't seem to connect the missing bracelet with the one I had bought, so I figured it was better to keep him in ignorance about that, just in case Dag was right and it was cursed. He was curse-happy enough without his girlfriend owning a cursed bracelet, not to mention possibly being the person who would put his twin in jail.

My mind went a bit squirrely at the word *girlfriend*, but I quickly brought it back to order, promising it that it could go squirrely later, after I'd dumped the bracelet. "Yeah. I thought if I break the fast once in a while, Allah won't get too mad at me, especially since I'm not a Muslim and all," I yelled back, as nonchalantly as I could.

"Absolutely," she bellowed. "Are you going to get a bottle of water?"

"Yup. Want one?"

She nodded, obviously tired of having to speak in such a loud voice. I signaled that I'd bring her one, and started the trek across the tent to where the bottled water was. Normally this wouldn't be a journey, but considering that the camp had been inundated with German tourists—important tourists, tourists who were paying a lot of money to mingle with real archaeologists on a real dig site—moving from one end of the mess tent to the other was like those nature films of salmon swimming upstream to spawn. Only I wasn't likely to squat over a convenient rock and lay eggs.

"The swimming—oh, sorry, didn't mean to step on you—upstream part is—ow! That was my kidney you just rammed your tray into!—pretty darn accurate. Cheese on rye, does everyone have to have lunch in here?"

I squeezed between German tourists, trying not to step on people or knock anyone's tray over, but it wasn't easy. The Germans were all excited, calling to one another, chatting, laughing, and generally getting in everyone's way. The tent was packed to capacity, with every bench taken. I grabbed two bottles of water and turned to make my way back to my spot. That's when I saw Chloe get up from her seat next to the door and push her way through the crowds to where another cooler was kept, this one holding soda pop.

The second she disappeared into the crowd I squeezed my way over to her spot, setting both bottles of water down and bending over as if I were going to tie my shoelace. I palmed the bracelet from my pocket, glancing around quickly to make sure no one was watching. The coast appeared clear, and as luck would have it, two Germans on the other side of the tent picked that moment to collide with a crash of trays and plates of food, as well as shrieks of laughing dismay. While everyone turned to look, I flipped up the napkin half tucked under a plate of chicken shawarma, and slid the bracelet under it.

No one saw as I grabbed the bottles of water and straightened up, moving off to my seat. It took a few minutes to reach it, since I had to detour around where the Germans were trying to scoop up broken plates and spilled food, but at last I made it back to my seat.

"Here's your water," I yelled at Izumi, handing her a bottle. "Boy, this is sure wild, huh?"

"Very wild," she agreed, taking a long swig of her water. I sat down and picked up my spoon, stirring the fruit salad, hoping everyone would believe I was eating. Daniel, one of the Copt diggers who sat on my other side, said something, but I couldn't hear it over the clamor.

When I leaned over to ask what he had said, a tourist behind me whacked my head with her tray, throwing me forward onto Daniel. My hand hit his just as he was taking a bite of fruit salad.

"Sorry," I yelled into his ear, giving the German tourist a glare as she walked on without apologizing.

"Is not problem," Daniel said.

I grabbed my napkin to wipe the fruit off my hand, but froze into a giant block of Jan as I stared at the object that sat on the tray, hidden by my napkin.

It was the bracelet. My bracelet. The one I'd just planted on Chloe's tray.

"Oh, my God, it *is* cursed," I whispered, looking it over without touching it. How could it be there? I had just hidden it on Chloe's tray. . . . Goose bumps rippled down my arm at that thought. It was in the exact same spot on my tray as where I had put it on Chloe's. Did I need any more proof that it was cursed? Maybe I was wrong in thinking Chloe had put it in my bag the night before. Maybe she had nothing to do with it. Maybe I had triggered some weird Egyptian curse by buying it, and now it was following me, returning to me every time I tried to get rid of it.

I fought down the urge to run from the tent screaming at the top of my lungs, and quickly covered the bracelet up with my napkin again. What was I going to do with it? How was I going to break the curse? And most important of all, how was I going to get rid of the stupid thing?

For a second, for a fraction of a second, for one of those nanoseconds that scientists are always flapping their lips about, for an infinitesimally small moment in time the wad of bodies in front of me parted and I looked straight down the tent to where Chloe sat. She had a strange look on her face, part disbelief, part horror, as her gaze met mine. Just as she opened her mouth to say something, the moment was lost and the tourists once again moved to block my view.

"Jan? Is anything wrong?" Izumi asked.

I jumped at her words, which had been gently bellowed into my ear, and without thinking grabbed the napkin-covered bracelet and stuffed it in my pants pocket. "No. Sorry. I have to go . . . uh . . . pee. Later!"

I hurried out of there as fast I could (which, considering the tourists, wasn't very fast at all). Once I managed to get out of the tent, I ran for the shady spot behind the equipment trailer. Seth wasn't there, which meant he had probably decided to hang out with the fasting workers. That was fine with me—I needed to have time to figure out what I was going to do about the bracelet.

"I thought you were going to have lunch?" a voice suddenly spoke behind me. For the second time in ten minutes I jumped up and shrieked.

"What, this is some sort of heart test or something?" I yelled at Seth. "You're trying to make sure I'm not going to go belly-up just because I'm hanging with you?"

"Sorry," he said, and sat down next to where I'd been standing. "I didn't mean to scare you."

"I thought you were over with your buds?" I glanced around before sitting down. The time had come to remind Seth about the bracelet, but I didn't want any witnesses in case he went psycho on me.

"I came back to see if you were finished." He took my hand and rubbed my fingers with his. My legs went all melty again, and I let inner Jan have a few seconds of giggling and feeling giddy just because I had lucked out and snagged the nicest guy in all of Egypt.

"I didn't exactly eat," I said, intending to tell him what happened with the bracelet, but before I could explain, he interrupted me.

"Jan, I want to say something to you. I admire you for

honoring Ramadan. I respect your right to make your own decisions. You're the smartest girl I know, and I wouldn't want you to change. I like all of you, every part, including your . . . uh . . ." His gaze dipped down to my chest. A wave of heat washed up from my neck as his eyes jerked back up to mine. "I don't want anything about you to change. All right? No more dieting."

I swallowed back a big lump in my throat and nodded, blinking like mad to keep the tears from spilling over. No one had ever said they liked me the way I was! Could he *be* any more perfect? "Okay. No dieting. But I'm still going to do the fast until Ramadan is over."

He groaned.

"I appreciate what you said, though. I . . . uh . . . I like everything about you, too."

He leaned forward to kiss me, but I stopped him by putting my fingers over his lips. "No."

"No?"

I traced a finger along the glossy line of his scrunched-up eyebrows. "No, as in not now. You have some sort of magic lips that make me forget whatever I was thinking when you kiss me, so no kissing until I've said what I want to say." I bit my lip as I scooted to the side. "It's about this."

He looked at the bracelet as I set it on his knee. "Your bracelet?"

"It's not mine," I said, taking a deep breath to try to calm myself. Just being near him made me feel so many things I didn't feel with other people, I had a hard time reminding my brain it should spend a little time thinking about things that didn't involve kissing Seth.

"It isn't?" The little gold flecks in the pretty brown part of his eyes sparkled. I leaned closer.

"No," I whispered against his lips, a goner. His magic lips won again.

"Whose is it?" he asked, one of his arms sliding around to my back.

"Whose is what?" I asked just seconds before I started kissing him. The heat of his mouth and the sweet touch of his tongue drove every thought from my mind but how much I liked kissing him. He pulled me over onto his lap, tipping his head back when I pulled on his ponytail. My fingers slid into the cool silk of his hair, working to untie the leather thong that held it back, slipping through the long black lengths of it when it was freed.

"I really like your hair," I murmured against his lips when we came up for air. "It's very sexy."

"I like yours, too," he said, wrapping a finger around a strand of my hair, pulling it straight and grinning when it snapped back to its normal curl. "It's red like the setting sun. Fiery. Exotic."

"Really? No one has ever thought I was exotic before," I said, giving him one more little kiss before pushing myself off his lap. He was way too sexy, and if I stayed curled up against him, I'd spend the whole lunch hour kissing him and not talking. "Seth, we have to talk."

He rubbed his thumb across my bottom lip. I'm lucky I was sitting down, because if I hadn't been, my legs would have collapsed. "About you being exotic?"

I shook my head and took a deep breath in an attempt to get a grip on myself. "No. We have to talk about that."

He glanced at the bracelet, now sitting on the ground next to him. "What about it?"

"You asked me who it belongs to. Well . . ." I gnawed on my lip for a second, remembering the heat of his mouth on mine. "It belongs to Mr. Massad."

Seth just looked at me for a minute; then he nodded. "I should have recognized it from the description. It's the stolen bracelet, isn't it? The one Dad calls—"

"The Handmaiden of Tekhnet, yes."

"Oh." His brows pulled together as he picked it up and gave it a once-over. "But you bought this in Cairo, at Hassad's shop."

"Exactly. Um . . . Seth, why were you in that shop?"

He shrugged, handing me back the bracelet. "We always go there. Hassad and Magdi are friends of my father."

It was my turn to frown. "Magdi?"

"The shop is really Magdi's. Hassan is the old man you saw, Magdi's father. He helps out at the shop occasionally. Magdi was gone the night we were in Cairo."

"Hmm, interesting," I said, tapping my lips with the bracelet until I realized what I was doing. Ick! Ancient Egyptian germs! Cursed ones at that! Blech!

"When you said *we*, you meant you and Cy?"

"Why are you asking all these questions, Jan?" he asked instead of answering.

I took another deep breath. "I'm investigating the theft. At first it was just so I could have a story, but now . . ." I gave the bracelet a wary look. "I think it wants me to find out who stole it, because . . . well, because it does seem to be cursed."

"How?" he asked, his voice hoarse.

"I . . . uh . . . Okay, this doesn't make me look very good, but you have to understand that Chloe is the one who started this. If she hadn't been flirting with you and kissing you, I never would have put it in her bed to begin with." It took five minutes, but I explained everything that had happened since I found out the bracelet was stolen. "And when I found it under my napkin a few minutes ago . . . well, what other reason could there be for it materializing there except that it really is cursed, and it wants me to find the person who stole it?"

He tugged on his lower lip for a second, making me think about how wonderful he tasted. "It just appeared there? No one was around you?"

"Nope. Seth, how often does Cy go into Magdi's shop?"

His brown eyes watched me carefully. "He didn't steal the bracelet."

I patted his arm. "I know he's your twin and all, but honestly, no one else had a reason to take it—"

"He didn't steal it." He shook his head, then ran one hand through his hair, pulling it back off his face. "I know you don't like him. I don't like him very much, but I do know him, Jan, and he wouldn't steal something. He doesn't have to—anything he wants, he gets."

"Yeah, but you said your parents didn't have enough money to send you both to college in America. Maybe he wanted something your dad couldn't afford . . ." A sudden image rose in my mind, an image of Cy playing a brand new electric guitar. "Something like a new guitar."

Seth's warm gaze met mine. He shook his head again. "He didn't steal the bracelet."

"When did he get the guitar? You said last night it was new, didn't you?"

"Yes." He looked away, his jaw tight. "He bought it a few weeks ago, in Cairo."

"The day after all of us Dig Egypt! kids arrived?"

He nodded, refusing to look at me.

I felt awful about making him realize the truth about Cy, but I had to do it. The bracelet wanted the person who stole it punished. And besides, it might open Seth's parents' eyes if they found out their precious, couldn't-do-any-wrong son was a thief.

"I'm sorry, Seth, I really am," I said, covering his hand with mine. He looked at me then, his long hair hanging like a silk curtain over his shoulders. "That night in Cairo, after dinner, I was on the balcony of the hotel, and I saw someone giving Cy a boatload of money."

"Who?" he asked, his voice deep with emotion.

"I don't know, but afterward, when I was sneaking back into the hotel, I saw one of the two blond guys you beat up in the alley. It had to be one of them."

"You're wrong about Cy, Jan, and I'm going to prove it."

I stood up when Seth did, my heart twisting with pain for him. I just wanted to hold him and keep him from being hurt, but I didn't know how I could protect him. "How are you going to prove it?"

"We're going to ask Cy where he got the money to buy the new guitar," he answered, taking my hand and hauling me after him toward the Muslim camp.

Oh, great. Just what I wanted—to confront Cy to his face, where he would say all sorts of mean things to me, and then Seth would hate me, and I'd lose the only guy I really, really liked, and my life would be over, and I wouldn't get my killer story. I dragged my feet as Seth pulled me toward the Muslim camp. "Couldn't you talk to him? You know, *alone?*"

"No. You need to be there. You need to see for yourself that he's not guilty." He stopped and frowned at me. I wanted to kiss his frown. "You want to be a journalist, don't you? This is the perfect opportunity for you to practice interrogating Cy."

"I already did."

He tugged me forward so I was walking next to him. "You said he tried to kiss you and you slapped him. You didn't ask him any questions."

"I didn't have to," I muttered.

"Yes, you do, and you know it."

I sighed and pinched his arm with my free hand. "Oh, all right, I'm willing to admit that maybe I was sure he did it before the interview, but you can't deny that what with him taking money from the blond guy who hit me in Cairo, he sure fits the role of suspect!"

"You'll see," was all Seth said.

I clammed up after that as well, figuring that the less I said, the better my chances were of emerging from the whole awful thing with my boyfriend intact.

Ten minutes later we found Cy. Five seconds after that, Seth punched his brother in the gut.

"That's for kissing my girl," he said calmly.

Cy grimaced as he rubbed his stomach, but didn't say anything other than nodding.

I glanced from him to Seth, surprised that not only would Seth be angry that Cy had tried to kiss me (he didn't sound mad at all when I told him) but also that Cy wasn't pissed that Seth had punched him.

"Did you just come here to do that, or was there something else you wanted?" Cy asked, sitting down on a blanket that was laid over the bare ground inside the tent.

Seth gestured toward the blanket. I sat down as well, wishing I had my notebook with me so I could make notes. I scooted closer to Seth when he plopped down on the edge of the blanket. "Where did you get the money to buy your new guitar?"

Cy's eyebrows rose. "Why do you care?"

It was weird sitting between the two of them. They looked so much alike, except now Seth's hair was loose, while Cy's was pulled back in a braid. Cy wore a muscle tee like Seth's, but in red. His black jeans were the same as his brother's, though.

"Jan thinks you're the person who stole that bracelet Dad said was missing."

"Hey!" I smacked Seth on the arm.

"You do think that," he said, giving me a frown. (What else was new?)

"Yeah, but you could have said that a lot nicer. Like by not including my name!"

"Jan, the whole reason we're here is because of you."

"I don't care; you could have phrased that better!"

Cy laughed, interrupting our argument. "You have it bad, don't you, little brother?"

Seth glared at him as I asked, "Have what?"

Cy grinned at me. Seth's cheeks turned a dusky red.

"Oh!" I said, my own face turning red as I looked

down at my hands. I was delighted and embarrassed at the same time by the thought of Seth being in love with me. It was a wonderful feeling, one I wanted to hug to myself and think about, but first I had to break Seth's heart by proving to him that his brother was a rat.

"Are you going to answer the question?" Seth asked.

"I will, but I don't have to," Cy told him. He turned to me, the smile still lurking in his eyes. "I was paid for delivering something to a shop in Cairo. I used that money to buy the Strat."

"What did you deliver?" I asked, wondering if he was telling the truth.

He shrugged. "I have no idea. It was fairly small, though."

Seth glanced at me, the gold flecks in his dark eyes shining brightly. "Something small, like a bracelet?"

"It might have been the bracelet," Cy said slowly, the smile fading from his eyes as he thought about it. He glanced at his brother. "Do you think it could have been?"

"Who did you deliver the package for?" I asked, my mind whirling. If it wasn't Cy, who was the thief?

"Dag."

I blinked a couple of times, my brain obviously in need of oxygen. "Dag?"

Seth reached for my hand, his fingers stroking mine as he narrowed his eyes at his brother. "Dag? Are you sure?"

Cy nodded. "She said she didn't have time to deliver it because she had to meet everyone at the airport. I figured it was one of her necklaces."

"Necklaces?" I asked, feeling a lot like a parrot.

Both guys nodded, but it was Cy who answered. "She makes bead necklaces and sells them to tourist shops. Or, at least, that's what she told us."

"Oh," I said, starting to believe him at last.

"Didn't you even look at what was in the package?" Seth asked, his fingers gentle on mine even though his voice was filled with disgust.

"Are you kidding? Why would I want to look at a bunch of ugly necklaces?" Cy made a face. "Not everyone is as suspicious as you are, little brother."

"It would have been better if you had been," Seth growled.

"What, and have people sticking snakes in my bed because they think I'm evil? No, thank you. One evil god in the family is enough."

"How did you know about the snake?" Seth asked, his fingers stilled, his dark eyes narrowed as they glared at his brother. "I didn't tell anyone but Jan about it."

I rubbed the top of his hand with my thumb. "And I didn't tell anyone."

Cy smiled and spread his hands wide. "It was just a joke, Seth. The snake wouldn't have hurt you—Zahi milked the venom from it before we put it in your room."

Seth said something that was probably swearing in Arabic as he lunged forward toward his brother.

"Wait!" I yelled as the two guys started rolling around the floor punching at each other. I jumped to my feet and kicked Cy on the leg. Hard. "We don't have time for this. If Dag is the one who gave Cy the bracelet to sell, that means she's the thief, but we'll need to find more proof."

Seth stood up, dusting himself off as Cy rolled up to a sitting position. He rubbed the spot on his shin I had kicked. "Proof? Why do you need proof? I just told you that she gave me a package to deliver."

"Yeah, but you didn't look in it, and it's just your word against hers." I turned to Seth, who was back to looking thoughtful, tugging on his lower lip as he watched me. "We need proof. Real proof. The most important thing is how Dag could have snatched the bracelet to begin with. How could she get into the artifacts trailer if it was locked and she didn't have the key?"

Seth's lips twitched for a second; then he grabbed my arms and pulled me up to his chest, bending over me like he was going to kiss me.

"Do you two have to do that in front of me?" Cy asked in a disgusted voice.

Seth's dark eyes were lit with victory. "You have a smut in your eye."

I blinked at him. "What?"

"A smut. You have a smut in your eye."

It slowly dawned on me what he was talking about. "Mr. Massad!"

Seth nodded.

"Dag is playing squishy-squishy with him, so that means she could have nabbed his key to the trailer and . . ." I paused for a minute, gnawing on my lip. "Could she have had a duplicate made?"

"In town. At the market."

I smiled as he let go of me. "Then that's proof, isn't it?"

"Almost. One of us should go into town tonight and

question the key makers." We both turned and looked at Cy, who was still rubbing his shin.

"Who, me? I don't want to go into town."

"You have to. Seth and I have other stuff to do tonight," I said, tugging Seth toward the door of the tent.

"Like what?" Cy asked, his normally smiley face in a pout.

I leaned forward and gave Seth a quick kiss before turning back to his brother. "Like arranging it so that Miss Dagmar Sorensson is caught blue-handed in front of the authorities!"

"Blue handed? I thought it was red-handed?" Cy's voice trailed after us as I dragged Seth after me.

MUMMY WREAKS VENGEANCE
BEYOND THE TOMB!

"Are you all coming for lunch?" Izumi looked up in surprise as Seth, Cy, and I filed into the mess tent the following day.

"Yeah. There's something we want to see." I glanced around the tent. Almost everyone who wasn't fasting was present, although I noted with irritation that Chloe, that Seth-kissing hussy, wasn't there. Neither was Connor.

"Really?" She looked past me to where Kay, Mr. Massan, Dr. Ray, and the armed guard all filed into the mess tent. "What's going on? Why do you have my sketchpad?"

"You'll see." I turned to Seth. "You're on next!"

He nodded, squeezed my hand, then went over to talk to his parents.

Cy sat down next to Izumi. "Did you know I could be a pickpocket if I wanted?" His fingers did their little waggle, and a coin appeared in them. "However, I've found that it's much harder to plant an object so someone will pick it up than it is to take something from them."

Something like the bracelet we'd treated, then placed

just outside Dag's tent door where she was sure to see it and pick it up on her way here, I mused to myself, watching Seth as he talked to his parents. He had wanted me to be the one to explain everything to them, but I had insisted that he take credit for figuring out the situation. His parents would see that he was serious about becoming an Egyptologist, so they'd find a way to send him to college in the United States along with Cy.

I really hoped so, because my heart was already breaking when I thought about having to go home without him.

"I am very busy now, Seth. There is much to do, and I cannot take the time to indulge you in a folly."

"It's not a folly," Seth told his father. "It's important. Please do this."

Dr. Ray looked like he was going to refuse, but in the end he sighed. "Everyone, might I have your attention, please?" He clapped his hands and shouted his request. Although the Germans had gone, the usual gang was pretty chatty at lunch, and it was hard to be heard over them. People stopped talking and looked over to where Dr. Ray was frowning at Seth.

"I can see where he got *that* trait," I said to myself.

"My son wishes to say something to you all," Dr. Ray said, evidently not happy. His lips were a thin line as he gestured toward Seth.

"What I have to say is about the curse of Tekhnet and Tekhen," Seth said, and everyone who had been whispering and giggling stopped dead.

Seth waved me forward. I peeled back the covering to Izumi's watercolor pad, flipping through it to the page I had painted the night before. I had begged Seth to do it, claiming his artistic skills had to be better than mine, but he insisted I try it. "Have you ever done a watercolor?" he had asked as we sat alone in the tomb, everyone else having gone to bed.

"No, but I don't need to try. I can't draw worth squat."

"You don't know what you can do until you try," he pointed out, and in the end I'd given in and copied a scene from the wall. It didn't turn out awful—you could see that what I had painted were Egyptian hieroglyphs and not just colorful blotches on the page—but it wasn't art.

"As you all know, the inscriptions on the wall in the upper chambers have already been translated," Seth said, looking around the mess tent to make sure everyone was listening to him. He didn't have to worry—people had stopped eating and were watching him carefully as he took the tablet of paper from me and held it up. "But the hieroglyphs on the lower levels, including the burial chamber, have not yet been translated. This painting, made by Jan James, is of a section in the burial chamber behind the sarcophagus."

He handed the tablet to his father. "I thought you might like to translate it here, Dad."

Dr. Ray gave his son a narrow-eyed look before taking the paper. I squirmed a little, worrying he was going to tell everyone the painting was so bad he couldn't understand the symbols, but he didn't. "It appears to be a warning of some sort," Dr. Ray said. "A curse, if you will, regarding the Handmaiden of Tekhnet."

I slid a glance to where Dag sat, a plate of lamb kebab in front of her. Her face was frozen, as if it were a Dag mask. I peeked at Mr. Massad, still not entirely sure that he wasn't helping his girlfriend to the dig goodies.

"Specifically, it says that he who removes the Handmaiden from Tekhnet's tomb will be struck by Set."

There was a hiss of breath as several people gasped and looked at Seth. I edged over to him and touched his hand with mine. He slid his fingers through mine, giving them a little squeeze. My heard did flip-flops, like it did every time he touched me.

"The god Set, lord of chaos, would strike the thief down by turning his hands, tongue, and feet blue so that all would know his perfidy."

Seth turned his head slightly and winked at me. I missed Dag's initial reaction because I was too busy grinning back at him, but as soon as she started shrieking curses at Seth, I turned back to watch the fireworks.

"Lies! The evil son is being telling of lies!" Dag screamed, standing up to hurl her accusations at Seth. "Pipples and childrens are not to be listening to cursed son! Curse of mummies dead is not that!"

"Really?" I asked, stepping forward, pulling in front of me the cloth bag that usually held my cleaning tools. "You're the one who is always saying there is a curse on stuff, Dag. Are you saying now that the bracelet *isn't* cursed?"

She looked confused for a second before her confusion turned into anger. "You! You are not knowing what talking about!"

"Ya think?"

"Seth is lying! You are his lady of bed. You are for him lying most horrible!"

Lady of bed? Oh! I put my hands on my hips. "I'm not doin' the nasty with anyone, not that it's any of your business."

She waved my objection away, shouting that Seth was evil, Seth lied, Seth was to blame for every bad thing that had happened at the camp.

"That's what you'd like everyone to believe," I said, moving back beside Seth. He put his arm around me. "But the truth is, he's just a convenient scapegoat, isn't he? It's called misdirection. You make everyone focus on Seth so they won't notice what's really going on."

"One moment, Jan," Dr. Ray interrupted me, holding up a hand to stop Dag. "I don't quite understand what it is you are saying, but I assume you are about to make an accusation against Dagmar. That is a very serious situation."

"More serious than the theft of antiquities?" I asked.

Dag gasped and hurled a bunch of Swedish at me. I figured it wasn't telling me how brilliant I was, so I ignored it.

Dr. Ray swapped glances with Kay, then turned to Seth. "What do you know about this?"

"Everything," I answered for him, grabbing the cloth bag. "Seth figured it all out."

Seth made a self-deprecatory move of his head. "Jan and Cy helped. We all figured it out together. Cy got the proof, while Jan and I arranged for this demonstration."

"Seth wrote the curse," I pointed out. "Without any training, yet! Wasn't that smart of him? Only a real Egyptologist could do that!"

Kay glanced at Dag. "What exactly is this demonstration?"

Seth gave me the nod to proceed. I pulled the small black object from the cloth bag and held it up.

"What are you doing with that?" Dr. Ray asked.

"Going to prove who the thief is, with Tekhnet's assistance," I said, clicking the small wand on. It hummed to life, a bluish-white glow coming from one length of it. "The curse reads that the thief's hands, feet, and tongue will turn blue."

Dag snarled something, then held her hands up palm-out for everyone to see. "It is not I who am having hands blue!"

"I didn't say you were the thief, did I?" I said sweetly, walking over to her. "But as you've volunteered, let's just see what Mr. Ultraviolet Scanner has to say about it."

I waved the scanner over her hands. Under the light, her right palm showed up a dark navy, as if stained by invisible ink.

"No!" she screamed, jerking her hand out from under the scanner. "It is not be! The Handmaiden is in my trunk most hidden. I have not touching it—oh! It was being the other!"

She stopped speaking as I reached out with two fingers and gently tugged the bracelet from the pocket of her khaki pants, right where Cy, Seth, and I had watched her place it a few minutes before. Our plan had gone like clockwork—Dag had found the bracelet where Cy had partially hidden it, and after glancing around quickly to see if anyone was watching, she had snatched it up and stuffed it in her pocket, getting the powder we'd spread all over the bracelet on her palm.

"Oh, really? So what are you doing with this?" I asked, holding the bracelet up so everyone could see it.

She screamed again and lunged at me, but Seth was there, holding her hands curled into claws as she tried to scratch me.

All hell broke loose then, with everyone jumping up, running around, talking, yelling, and asking for explanations. By the time the guard was leading her away, she was borderline manic. Dr. Ray stared at Seth like he'd never seen him before, while Kay beamed at everyone. "Weren't they clever? I had no idea last night why Jan and Seth were asking about the fluorescent powder we use to show hairline cracks in the tomb walls, but it was very smart of them to put that knowledge to such good use."

I wrapped my fingers around Seth's. "It's smart unless the police don't find any proof that she's really guilty, and then it's . . . uh . . . what is it?"

"Entrapment," Seth said, his fingers tightening around mine.

Mr. Massad came in from Dag's tent at that moment, shaking his head as he held out his hand. On it lay the Handmaiden. "It will not be entrapment."

My mouth dropped open as I looked from the bracelet in his hand to the bracelet lying on the table. "There's two of them? Two Handmaidens of Tekhnet?"

"Twin bracelets for twin manicurists," Dr. Ray said, his voice full of pleased surprise. "It makes sense."

"I knew there were two mummies, but I didn't know they were *twins*. Imagine that," I said, grinning up at Seth. He grinned back at me, his wonderful eyes sparkly and bright with a look that left me feeling warm all over.

Cy wandered over, giving the two of us a sour look. "You're going to start kissing again, aren't you?"

"Yes," Seth said, and pulled me out to the nearest tent. "How do you feel, January James? You've caught the thief, cleared my name, and proved you can paint—three miraculous accomplishments in less than a month!"

I wrinkled my nose, then leaned forward and nipped at his lower lip. "I'm just happy about my best accomplishment."

"What's that?" he asked, his voice like velvet as his arms wrapped around me.

I slid my hands up his back and kissed each corner of his mouth. "I got the guy, silly!"

THIEF CAUGHT AT LUXOR DIG

(LUXOR): last week officials from the Supreme Council of Antiquities announced that an arrest had been made in the thefts of various antiquities uncovered in the tomb of Tekhnet and Tekhen, twin manicurists to Queen Nefertari. Mr. Gaballah Massan, Undersecretary of the Department for Egyptology, was on the site when the thief, Dagmar Sorensson of Stockholm, Sweden, was arrested.

"We are shocked, deeply shocked," Mr. Massan said when questioned about the identity of the thief. "This dig has been plagued with thefts of minor pieces for the last six months, all of which we now know were carried out by Dag . . . er . . . Miss Sorensson and her two brothers. Miss Sorensson's method was to confiscate an item, carry it to Cairo, and there dispose of it in a small shop, claiming it was a reproduction."

An American teen working at the Tekhnet dig site stumbled onto the truth about the thefts when she inadvertently purchased one of the stolen objects. According to the Cairo police, the shop owner was promised a reward if he sold the objects only to individuals who mentioned the Valley of the Servitors, the Sorenssons' code phrase. The object was then resold on the black market, providing Miss Sorensson with distance should the police have tracked it to the shop and connected it with her.

"Naturally all three Sorenssons will be prosecuted to the fullest extent our laws allow," Massan added. "I believe I speak for everyone when I say how profoundly shaken we are to find a member of Dr. Tousson's highly respected dig team a thief."

Key in discovering the identity of the thief was Seth Tousson, who uncovered the facts leading to the identity of the culprit.

"Once we put together the facts, there was only one person it could be," Seth said when asked how he came to the conclusion that the Dig Egypt! volunteer coordinator was guilty. "She tried to confuse everyone by claiming there was a curse haunting the site, blaming me for everything that happened, but in the end, she was the one who suffered."

Tousson, eighteen and incredibly sexy with long black hair and pretty eyes with gold flecks, smiled and added, "I couldn't have done it without my girlfriend, Jan. She's the one who really started the investigation. Cy and I just helped her."

When asked what he was going to do with the reward of thirty-five thousand piastres for the arrest of the antiquities thief, Tousson grinned. "I'm going to use the money to study at the University of Chicago. My brother will be there as well, but the best part is that Jan lives just a few hours away in Wisconsin, so we'll be able to see each other on weekends and holidays. She's the best thing that has ever happened to me—I'd be lost without her."

Reported by January James, guest correspondent and girlfriend to a god.

Don't miss Chloe's side of the story in

by Naomi Nash

Turn the page for a sneak preview!

One

Across barren sands an oasis waited for me, green and cool and shimmering with water. Sunlight made the dunes painfully bright, but my slitted lids held no moisture. Only two miles to go, and I could drink long and deep. "Water!" I croaked, but no one was there to hear me.

Then I heard a voice whispering my name. "Chloe."

Hold on. Was I hallucinating? Or was I already dead? I'd been told that people lost in the desert sometimes heard things . . . right before they went totally insane. I shook my head, hoping the motion might jar out the voice. Where had it come from? Behind me was only my shuffled trail in the sand, which even now was being erased by desert winds hotter than the ground underfoot. Ahead of me was nothing but wasteland. And above, Egypt's white-hot sun, blazing down as if it wanted to burn from the landscape any trace of me it could find. *You're going to die here,* I told myself. *You should never have stepped foot in this most ancient of lands. You're a fake.*

I shook my head again. No. I had absolutely no intention of dying here. I had not come all the way from Seattle to collapse in the wilderness, my corpse picked over by buzzards, with no grave other than the shifting sands. The oasis was only two miles away, and there I could quench my thirst with water, sweet water. . . .

"Chloe." I heard the voice again. "Chloe! Wake up!"

For, like, a split second after I opened my eyes, I was convinced my friends had rescued me from certain death in the middle of Egypt's endless sands. But no. I seemed to be in a dark space, lying on a cot that had transformed my butt into a lumpy sack of potatoes. I hadn't been saved at all. I had been sleeping. When I licked my cracked lips, I realized how thirsty I was. No wonder my dreams were of the desert.

No. Wait. The past week came flooding back to me. I *was* in the desert. In Egypt. The Valley of the Servitors, working on the tomb of Tekhen and Tekhnet, to be precise.

The four-letter word that came flying out of my mouth was one everyone in my family had used at some time or another, but it wasn't one I usually said louder than a whisper. My tentmate, Sue Chatterjee, must have heard it, though, because her face suddenly appeared over the tips of my toes. "I know!" she said.

Huh? That didn't make sense. And what was she doing down there?

"But Chloe . . . don't move, okay? It'll be all right." Sue's brown eyes stretched wide with fear and concern. She had a habit of gnawing on the tip of her big, dark braid whenever she was nervous, but now she was practically sucking the color right out of it.

"I'm okay," I said sleepily. What time was it? Was I late for breakfast? "I was only dreaming."

When I tried to sit up in my cot, Sue pointed at my stomach and screamed loudly enough to shatter glass, "Don't move!"

I froze and scrunched up my face. Okay, who substituted crazy powder for her Tang this morning? There was nothing on me except for a little woven bracelet someone had left there. It was kind of pretty, all stripes of black and greenish brown with fringy bits. . . .

To my horror, the bracelet lifted its fringy bits and began to crawl in my direction. That was no jewelry. A scorpion was slowly making its way across my blanket! When suddenly I sucked in a lungful of air, the scorpion stopped, quivering its tail as if it were about to strike.

Don't move? The *heck!* Somehow I think—and I bet about 99 percent of the world population would agree with me on this—that when a girl wakes up and sees a scorpion perched on her belly, moving is the first thing she wants to do! I peered at Sue over my blanket's edge, my heart pounding so furiously that it seemed to be flopping around the inside of my mouth. For the first time I noticed the other Dig Egypt! kids crowded outside around the tent flap, all of them watching me. None of them was doing a thing. Oh, no, that would be too helpful. They all merely stood there, looking at me as if I were dead already.

Over my racing pulse, my brain registered how annoyed I was at that.

Three nights ago, right after our arrival at the camp, the archaeologist in charge of excavation had presented a long lecture on desert-survival tactics. Between her warnings on snakes, insects, disease, rabid dogs, and emergency terrorist evacuation procedures, she'd so badly scared the six of us on the excavation team that we all wished we still wore diapers.

Desperately my mind chugged away while I tried to remember vital information that was coming back to me only in dribs and drabs. Okay, Dr. Battista had said there were green African scorpions and black African scorpions. One of them was bad news, the other not so much. But which was which? Black for bad? Green for poison? This was important stuff here, so why wasn't I remembering anything she'd said?

Oh, yeah. Maybe because the adults in charge decided to give us all that lifesaving information immediately after I'd spent twenty-one hours on airplanes from Seattle to New York to Paris to Cairo, followed by a bumpy drive in vans from Cairo to Luxor, so that I'd felt like a zombie extra from *Night of the Living Dead,* that's why.

Smart, folks. Real smart. I cursed whoever it was who'd had *that* bright idea.

Meanwhile, the scorpion certainly wasn't hailing a taxi and toddling off for a night at the opera. On pointed claws it marched up the blanket, readying its tail to strike after every one of my shudders. I was going to die, right here and now, just like in my dream. The only way I would get home from Egypt would be in a body bag. Thanks bunches, Mom and Dad!

No. Nuh-uh. Not this time. I absolutely refused to die unshowered and in my sleepwear. "Sue," I said in a soft voice that sounded much calmer than I felt. "Sunita!" I snapped, using her full name. Sue seemed more concerned with calming Deidre Pierce—the camp coward, who whimpered and sobbed while the arachnid tried to find the ideal spot to impale me—than with my immediate demise. Now, how could I remember that scorpions were arachnids and not insects, but I couldn't figure out whether I was about to require an airlift to a hospital or just an ice pack and some aspirin? Life was just *so* unfair sometimes.

"Sorry," said my tentmate. "Deidre's pretty scared."

"*Deidre's* scared!" The heck! "Clear the others away. I'm going to do something." I bet neither kid on the restoration team, both snug in their real beds in a converted monastery house miles away, had to deal with this kind of crap.

"I got a shout out for Dag," I heard Bo call from outside. "Just keep cool."

"Ms. Sorensson is coming," Sue echoed. "She'll know what to do." Then, to the girl at her other side with the short-bobbed dark hair, she added, "*Le*, um, how do you say, *est arrivant*. What's 'chaperone' in French?"

Oh, fine. I was about to meet my maker while Sue translated my plight to our Parisian student. " 'Chaperone' *is* French, Sunita!" I yelled at her.

I was sunk. Our flaky chaperone would take one look at the scorpion and run in the opposite direction. On second thought, the scorpion might take a look at Dagmar Sorensson and scamper away, scared for its life. Still, it wasn't a chance I wanted to take. "I'm not waiting for that redheaded clown," I barked back. Immediately I noticed how strained and strange my voice sounded. Could they hear it too?

"Please please please please please don't do anything, Chloe." For the first time in my life, I actually saw someone bite her lip and wring her hands. The only thing keeping Sunita from being the overacting heroine of a silent movie was a big old villain with a waxed mustache tying her to railroad tracks. "That scorpion could kill you! *La mort,*" she added for Mallorie Dupuis.

The French girl gasped. *"La mort!"*

All rightie, then. That settled that! Black must be the bad kind.

"Okay," I said aloud. "You . . . just . . . stay . . . calm." I didn't know whether I was talking to myself or to the scorpion. Maybe a little of both. "I'm going to . . . That's it." I slid my hands from under the covers to the top of the blanket until the scorpion suddenly paused. Did they have noses? I didn't think so. Still, it looked as if it was sniffing in my direction. "That's right," I told it, swallowing heavily. "Be still."

Thank goodness I had tucked in the bottom of my blanket the night before—in case some bug or mouse or snake had decided to crawl up under it, in fact. Fat lot of good that had done to keep deadly bugs—*arachnids,* whatever—from setting up shop on my vital regions. My foresight had given me a perfect anchor for the blanket, though. I began to lift the rough covering up and away from my body.

Outside the tent, Deidre Pierce shrieked as simultaneously the scorpion suddenly dashed two inches in the direction of my face. Annoying, that. "Too fast," I told myself, slowing down my movements. "It's okay, little scorpion." I kept my voice down to a whisper, aware that everything was so quiet around me now that I could hear the chatter of the cooks and the sound of clashing dishes from the mess tent, halfway across the camp. "It's okay." With some extremely gradual lifting, I managed to raise the blanket a good three or four inches from my body. The scorpion stayed very, very still.

While I eyed the creepy-crawly, I pulled myself up to a sitting position, holding the blanket as motionless as possible. There was a tense moment when it began to pull away from one of the corners, but within a few seconds I was able to swing my feet over the cot's edge. No mean feat, considering how trembly my legs felt.

"Okay." I used my singsong voice, very softly. "Is everyone away from the flap? Because I'm going to get rid of this very nice . . . sweet . . . good scorpion." By now I'd managed to ease myself to my feet, the top edge of the blanket still in my hands. The only way the thing could hurt me now was if it jumped at my face. They couldn't do that, could they? Could they jump? Only Mexican beans jumped, right? Maybe I didn't want to know.

I heard noises from the other kids when I shifted myself around so that I faced the bed, but all my attention was focused on the deadly little bundle of sharp pointy bits and venom circling the middle of the cot. With my left hand I tugged the far end of the blanket from the bottom of the bed frame until it was completely loose. "Okay," I said, ignoring the slight shake in my voice. The kids would panic if I didn't make myself sound calm. "Everyone stand clear." I held my breath. This was it.

"Now!"

I grabbed the four corners of the blanket and, holding it as far away from my body as I could, stooped and ran out under the tent flap. My wrist banged against the center tent pole on the way out, and my bundle with it. I didn't stop running, though. Like I was going to open up the blanket before I had to? Hardly. Still, I felt a twinge at the thought that I might have smashed my little passenger. Aquarians like me didn't get along with Scorpios, generally, but I hated crushing bugs. I couldn't even kill a spider. This was kind of the same thing as getting rid of a spider outdoors, right?

As fast as my legs could take me, I ran and ran to the edge of camp, where the slope ended in a sharp drop to the canyon below. Pebbles cut into the soles of my feet, but I didn't care. At any other time I would've grudgingly admired the sight of the ancient catacombs carved into the cliffs below, almost colorful against the sunrise. With a lethal critter in tow, however, let's just say I was not in a rosy early-morning mood. I flung out the blanket over the edge of the cliff as if I were shaking the dust and sand from it. "Buh-bye!" I yelled after the scorpion, expecting my gesture to send it sailing out into the air and over the cliff.

Only nothing flew out.

Oh, crud. I dropped the blanket on the ground. Against its gray weave I saw no trace of scorpion. No scorpion goo from being banged against the tent pole. Nothing. Gingerly I grabbed one of the corners and flung it over. Nothing there, either. But then where . . . ?

"Chloe!" one of the Tousson twins called out in his deep voice from the camp's edge. When I turned, all the Dig Egypt! kids were watching me. For the first time I noticed that most of them still wore the T-shirts and sweats that we all used for nightclothes. Sue must have roused them straight out of their beds. "Behind you!"

I followed the direction of the Tousson twin's finger. I'll be darned if the little fiend wasn't skittering in my direction, hell-bent on plunging its twitchy stinger into the fleshiest part of me it could find. I was so startled by its velocity that my legs instinctively jerked as I yelped and jumped . . .

. . . and side-kicked the scorpion right over the slope edge. I barely felt it brush my toes as it went flying out into the air. It was with amazement that I watched it fall and disappear beyond the rock beneath our feet. Wait a minute! *I* did that?

"Whoa!" said Bo, running forward.

"Mon Dieu!" Mallorie jogged up beside me and looked over the side of the cliff.

I peered over too. *Mon Dieu,* all right. It was goner than gone. Score one for scorpion kickball!

Before I even realized what I'd done, I was surrounded by the other kids. One of the twins—I still had a hard time telling Seth apart from Cyrus—was clapping me on the back. Someone was picking up my blanket and folding it. Several more were congratulating me. In my thudding head I couldn't even distinguish the gabble into words, but I knew I didn't deserve a word of it.

When my eyes cleared and I looked back to camp, I found the path blocked by Kathy Klemper and, looming behind her, Dagmar Sorensson. Dag wore a head of curly red hair cut into an unfortunate wedge I hadn't seen since I stumbled across some of my mom's more painfully embarrassing record albums from the eighties—Dag looked so much like a fast-food clown that we called her "Rona McDonald" behind her back. Well, that's what I called her. It had kind of caught on among the excavation team kids, though.

It was obvious ol' carrottop had been giving some new kid a fifty-cent tour of the archaeologist's camp. He trailed behind her with his suitcase, shoulders slumped, his face hidden beneath his baseball cap.

Even though the rest of us still wore our sleepwear, Kathy was already in her khakis. Her tight ponytail hung down in a perfect tress at the back of her head. Don't ask me how she kept so tidy—after three days of not washing it, my short black hair was a greasy mess of tangles and snarls that I kept concealed with a bandanna most of the day. Kathy's expression was so spiteful that you could have collected it in fancy spray bottles and sold it as Calvin Klein's Utter Disdain. "There she is," she said in one of those voices that could curdle wet concrete. "Did you see, Ms. Sorensson? Chloe *kicked* local fauna over the cliff." I'd known I hated Kathy three hours into the project; three days in and I wished she'd been the one I'd kicked.

Just the month before in tenth-grade English I'd read a short story about a guy named Dorian Gray who never seemed to grow older, though the painting of himself he'd stuffed in his attic practically collected Social Security checks. I had a private theory that Dag had some kind of similar deal going on with her laundry. Her uniforms never wrinkled or grew dirty, but somewhere in someone's attic was a basket filled with filthy clothes that smelled like rotting corpses with a twist of skunk. I suspected Dag was using more water than her ration. "Chloe Bryce!" she snapped.

I tried not to watch her wedge of orange hair bob atop her head as she stomped over. "How many times I am telling you? Little birds and bees of the desert regions of Egypt are *not* to be made the trampling upon. We are being guests here. We tread with the light foot!" Dagmar's Swedish accent always made me feel as if I were lurching around in a roller coaster.

"My foot *are* the light foot!" I protested ungrammatically. She made it sound like I made a habit of drop-kicking every Egyptian bird, bug, and mammal I saw! "That scorpion trampled on me!"

"If it makes the trampling on you, it is from you disturbing the tomb of the dead," Dagmar proclaimed. For someone who worked at an archaeological site, she had a weird superstitious streak. "It is curse! You will be being dead from bite of scorpion!"

When Kathy Klemper had the nerve to smirk, I muttered with no little bitterness, "Sounds like you'd be happier if I died of a scorpion bite."

"I am hearing nonsense," Dag continued. "I am your chaperone, yah? Here to be ensuring safety and happiness for all childrens?" Once she'd volleyed that lie, she launched into an address that was intended to cow me with its volume and intensity. Respect for wildlife, check. Stupid blathering about curses, check. Reminders that she was the authority here and I was a mere child, check. General snottiness designed to make me feel like a dung ball a scarab might roll, check, check, check all the way to the bottom of the page. By the speech's end my head was reeling. It was also starting to feel a little baked as the Egyptian sun inched its way over the top of the mess tent.

"Got it," I said when she took an opportunity to breathe. "You betcha, coach."

Oops. Wrong word. I could tell as soon as it left my mouth. Her left eyebrow flew up as if it were counterweighted to a heavy pulley. "Chaperone," she said in a tone chipped out of dry ice. "Now is time to be dressing. We have full day ahead. You, new young boy, I show you to your tent," she added. The new kid stood behind her, shifting his weight under his heavy backpack. An iPod was strapped to his waist, but its small earphones had been tucked into a pants pocket. The boy had been staring at me all through Dag's speech, but it was only at that moment that I once more noticed him.

When our eyes met, I stood still, stunned. My flesh had turned to stone.

"Well, I think it's terrible that Rona McDonald's always on your case," said Sunita, watching the chaperone stir up clouds of dust on her march back to camp. "And that Kathy Klemper is a snitch. You know how she got here? Her father's one of those University of Seattle professors, that's why."

"So's mine," I told her, barely able to work out the words. I couldn't tear my gaze from the boy's brown eyes. Curly brown hair spilled from under his backward-facing baseball cap onto the nape of his neck. "Oh, my God," I whispered. It was Connor Marsh. Connor Marsh was here in Luxor? And there I was, looking like . . . oh, man. Probably awful, in my sloppy sweats and my short black hair hanging every which way.

Deidre Pierce stepped in front of me, her thick dark eyebrows scrunched together in the middle, momentarily obscuring my view. "I wish I were like you," she admitted to me, hugging herself tight. "I just get *scared* of stuff like that. Why don't you ever get *scared?*"

Her words stabbed right to my gut. I couldn't let it show, though. "Aw, heck, it's nothing really."

Bo Mereness clapped me on the back so hard that I

nearly followed the scorpion over the cliff. He always talked to me like I was some kind of local hero. "Clo-meister! That was even better than when you were, like, the only one who crossed that humongous burial shaft when we went on that tour the first night. Remember? You're amazing!"

Remember? How could I forget? I could have been living a life of luxury down at the old monastery with the kids on the conservation team if I hadn't been the only Dig Egypt! kid to sprint across a two-by-four laid across the dark shaft on our first night. It was only when I looked back and saw none of the other kids following me that I realized I'd done something unusual. "She's supposed to be with conservation? No way—she's definitely one of ours," archaeologist Eddie Loret had said to Anca Battista, despite the fact that I wanted to scream at the thought of being on the excavation team for the rest of my stay.

The twins were sons of the project's rarely seen director, Dr. Tousson. They helped out the conservation team. I had twin brothers at home who were an awful lot alike, but these guys were uncannily similar—twin hunks who'd both gotten more than their share of the hottie gene. Mmmm, had they ever! I think I was catching on to the trick of telling them apart, though. Cyrus was the dark-skinned eighteen-year-old sex bomb with the thick eyebrows and long hair and the buffed-out chest and white, white teeth and sexy smile whom all the adults adored; he was supposed to be a genius of some kind. Seth was the dark-skinned eighteen-year-old sex bomb with the thick eyebrows and long hair and the buffed-out chest and white, white teeth and sexy smile who was supposed to be the bad boy of the two. Apart from each other, they were impossible to distinguish. "You are not like most American girls," said He-Who-I-Thought-Might-Be-Cyrus. I hoped it was a compliment. I wanted to melt at his smile, at his long braid, and at his beautiful, beautiful brown eyes. "You are . . . extraordinary."

Even the way he said *extraordinary* sounded extraordinary. "Oh, it's nothing," I said, bluffing it off and hoping he didn't notice my blush. Having Cyrus so much as notice me was making my insides squirmy. I mean, it even hurt to look at the guy, he was so hottilicious. Why hadn't I stopped to put on some lip gloss before I left the tent? Stupid, stupid Chloe!

He bowed his head at me and walked away. " 'Bye . . . Cy," I said, not saying the name very loudly. Had that been Cyrus? Or Seth? While I watched him go, I craned my neck to catch sight of Connor again. I could see only the back of his T-shirt, though, splashed with a big number 2, as he followed Dagmar and Kathy Klemper.

"Nothing!" said Bo. "You lie! That was ab-so-frickin'-lutely ab-so-mazing!"

"That twin is so seriously gorgeous," Deidre whispered. "I would have *fainted* if he talked to me."

She wasn't kidding. She really would have fainted. "Which one was he?" I asked her.

"Ohmigod, who cares?" Sue whispered to me. "He *talked* to you!" To Mallorie she explained, "*Le bel homme a parlé à mon mate du tent!*" Mallorie looked as dubious as ever.

The five of us started shuffling our way back to camp. The sounds of people rousing themselves and getting ready for a day's work were louder now. The rusty water tank was creaking ominously, the way it did when its water supply got low—which was always. And over it all I could smell sausages for breakfast.

I wasn't hungry at all, though. I couldn't even stomach the thought of food, or of washing the grit from my face with the half cup of water I'd be allotted for the day. All I could think about was Connor—a boy I already knew. Who was from my school. Who was only a grade ahead of me.

And who was going to bring everything I'd hoped to change about myself crashing down around me? Connor Marsh. Because the voice in my dream had been dead right. I was a total and utter fake, and he was the one person who would know it.

Didn't want this book to end?

There's more waiting at **www.smoochya.com**:

Win FREE books and makeup!
Read excerpts from other books!
Chat with the authors!
Horoscopes!
Quizzes!

 Bringing you the books on everyone's lips!